MOIST

MOIST

EBONY ETHERIDGE

authorHOUSE®

AuthorHouse™
1663 Liberty Drive
Bloomington, IN 47403
www.authorhouse.com
Phone: 1-800-839-8640

First published by AuthorHouse   02/13/2012

ISBN: 978-1-4685-5374-1 (sc)
ISBN: 978-1-4685-5375-8 (ebk)

Printed in the United States of America

INTRODUCTION

I've gotten a lot of questions about Moist. Mostly questions asking if this is truth or fiction. I always tell them that art imitates life and life imitates art.

This is a fiction novel and the way it came to life was from a good friend of mine by the name of Karen Williams.

She and I met at the University of Miami and instantly connected. She would often tell me that she knew I had a book in me just waiting to come out.

We would e-mail each other back and forth daily. Then one day I came up with the characters JaLisa and Richard and the story came to life.

Ebony Etheridge

PLEASE BE ADVISED THAT THIS BOOK WILL
WORK WONDERS FOR THE LIBIDO. :-)

~ JALISA ~

It's my first day at the University of Miami and I'm thirty minutes late for my Journalism class. "Shit," I mumble to myself as I walk into the over sized lecture hall. All these rich bitches staring up in my damn face like I don't belong here. They got their nerve, the only reason they're here is cause their daddies are rich. My heart is pumping and my panties are moist. Richard gave me a ride to school today but he insisted that we had to stop at his place first. My thoughts are interrupted by this thunderous voice.

"You must be JaLisa Wright!" Mrs. Brooks the professor said as I tried to tip toe to an empty seat near the back of the lecture hall.

I'm guessing she knew me by name because I'm the only one that didn't answer when she did roll or I am the only black girl with a ghetto name.

"Yes Ma'am, I apologize for being late but I was having car trouble . . . You have my word that it won't happen again."

"I'd rather if you not sit in the back row there is an empty seat right here in the front." She said with a coy smirk.

Before I could climb over the white chicks and make it to the front and center seat she had already placed the class syllabus on my new chair. I felt as if I was in grade school but that's exactly what I get for getting a quickie before class.

This syllabus is heavy as shit. It's pages and pages of instructions on what we are going to be doing this semester. Mrs. Brooks turns to the board and begins to talk and write explaining that we need to take sufficient notes and that nothing will be repeated.

"There will be groups of two and this will be your partner the remainder of the semester. If your partner decides to drop this class for any reason you are left to carry the load on your own."

"Do I make myself clear?"

No one answered out loud we all just nodded in agreement. As the groups started pairing up I fell into a day dream drifting to the thought of Richard with my clit ring between his gold teeth. I don't know what I see in him, he's six years younger than I but I've never had any other person male or female make my legs shake the way he does. And he's so romantic my body gets chills just thinking of the way he flips his tongue.

This Spanish chick and I are the only ones that haven't chosen partners so of course we are stuck with each other. This bitch has much attitude and I am not impressed one bit. She holds out her hand with a vague expression on her face and says, "Hey, my name is Consuela."

"And I'm JaLisa but you already knew that since I came in so late."

"You didn't miss much just the dos and donts and number one was don't be late."

"Like I said I had car trouble."

"Uh huh," she said rolling her eyes.

"Okay your first assignment is to do an interview on your partner. The interview needs to be done as if you are a newswriter." Mrs. Brooks left the lecture hall after that she said she needed to go run off copies of an assignment that we are to do before the next class meets.

Consuela pulled out her spiral notebook and said, "Let's get this over with." Just as she said that I received a text message on my cell phone from Richard. *CAN I C U AFTA CLASS.*

I quickly type back *HELL NO YOU GOT ME IN TROUBLE!*

My phone starts vibrating again *I JUS WANNA EAT IT RAW.*

My eyes lit up and my panties are moist again. Consuela interrupts my thought process when she asked the first interview question.

"Where were you on December 1st?"

"What?"

"Just answer the question you are the prime suspect in your boy friends murder."

Jokingly I pled the Fifth Amendment.

"Okay look if we are going to pass this semester we are going to have to take it seriously my interview is with a young woman that is the prime suspect in her boyfriend's murder and it is my job to find a motive."

"I . . . uh was at the hair dresser in the 183rd flea market on December 1st." I said as I throw my braids over my shoulder.

"What time were you there from?"

"I was there from nine in the morning till about 2pm, I got my braids done and they always take forever to do my braids."

Consuela looked at me and again rolled her eyes.

"What's the name of your stylist? We will have to question her as well?"

"Her name is Brea Russell."

"How long have you known your now deceased boy friend Thomas Peterson?"

"We've dated on and off for the past two years but I met him three years ago at the same flea market where I got my braids done."

"Okay so we have an alibi from the hours of nine to 2pm, but where were you once you left the hair salon? According to the autopsy it shows that Mr. Peterson died five hours earlier from the time he was found which would have been at about 4pm."

"Well I . . . I got my braids done like I said, then I went home. I was tired after all that time in the salon."

Consuela burst out laughing, "Girl you tripping."

When I walked out to the Stanford Circle to wait on the shuttle bus I heard Richard's horn blowing. I started to hop on the first shuttle that I saw passing by but my body wouldn't allow me it wanted to finish what we had started earlier. The sun glared off his gold teeth as he reached over to open the passenger door. My clit is starting to pulsate for him.

Damn what have I gotten myself into? I really love the way he looks out for me.

"I told you not to pick me up!"

"Baby you know I had to see you," he leans back over and kissed me on my neck.

"I can't be late to class anymore Richard that professor was on my ass today!"

"Okay love, my place or yours?"

He is totally ignoring me. He always does this when I let him have it. He is going to have to work extra hard this evening.

Instead of going to his place I tell him to take me home and of course I act as if I have an attitude. Richard is sounding like Keith Sweat: "There you go telling me no again."

"Baby please don't be mad at me. Let me make it up to you."

I walk out of the car and slam the door in his face and he jumps out. He is starting to look vexed but there is nothing he can do. This is just my way of having mind control I know exactly what buttons to push because I am older than he is. He's used to dealing with these young ass girls that live with their Mamas and have no sense of direction. This time he is dealing with a woman and don't know what I have planned next.

"Richard, look you can come in but you are not staying over tonight I have to be at work early in the morning and don't have time to be late for that too."

His feelings are hurt but oh well I have to set some boundaries or he will be trying to move into my shit. We walk into my place and the smell of my Glade Plug In hits us in the face. It smells so delicious. Or maybe it's because I haven't eaten all day.

"Richard, make yourself at home I am going to get comfortable you know where everything is."

He plops down on the sofa and reaches for the remote. I recently had Satellite installed so that seems to take him out of his funk. He goes straight to those damn videos with the hoochies all shaking their asses.

"Whateva!" I slam the door to the bathroom behind me.

I allow the hot steam from the shower message my entire body. I reach for my Victoria's Secret Love Spell shower gel and the bottle crashed to the floor.

"You alright in there," he yells.

I don't even reply I take the sponge and massage my shoulders with the lathered sponge. I love this smell. I take the sponge and rub each nipple slowly as they become erect. I feel myself getting moist. I allow the suds to run down my stomach to my pubic hairs and to the front of my thighs . . . this is so great. I inhale and exhale the aroma of the Love Spell and I know it's about to be heated Richard loves this stuff. Lifting one leg on the side of the tub I lather it then the other. My shower is almost over but not before I slide my fingers down and rub my clit. I allow the hot steam to run the suds off and my shower is over. I don't even bother to dress I just rub my body down with baby oil while I'm still soaking wet and I dab myself dry with the towel. The steam is pouring out the bathroom when I open the door. "Damn did you have the water hot enough in there?" I started to get smart but my Glade Plug In smell is replaced with the aroma of a personal Tortilla extra cheese pizza that I had in the freezer. Richard must have been reading my mind. While I was taking a shower he made us some personal pizzas and he cut mine into four slices and had it on a plastic plate so I wouldn't have to wash any dishes. He also made me a glass of Vodka with grapefruit juice, just like I like it. My attitude instantly fades and I'm rather impressed. He must have figured that I hadn't eaten yet. When I sat down I still had my towel wrapped around me. He stood behind me and massaged my shoulders. He told me to press play on the remote to the five disk CD changer. The first song is from Destiny Child's CD "Cater 2 U." I love this song. He is so romantic in a thuggish type of way. My nipples are showing through my towel. I want to jump his bones but he makes me sit and eat while he continues to relax me by massaging my shoulders. I take a sip of the Vodka and it's just right. Not too much liquor but lots of grapefruit juice. Once I finish eating and my drink is gone he reached down and unwrap the towel when the next song starts to play from Usher's Confession CD. The song "That's what it's made for" is playing.

He takes my left hand and I get up from the table. He picks me up and I'm shocked because I'm a little thick in the thighs and he places me on the kitchen counter. Now this is something I've always wanted to do but never had it done. Richard starts eating my p---- like I am a main course. I guess that little box pizza did nothing for him. All you can hear is Usher singing and Richard slurping.

"Oh Shit Richard, right there baby!"

I throw my head back and it hits the cabinet. He tells me just as Usher tells the woman at the end of the song, "that was only the beginning." The next song plays and its still Usher "Can you handle it." Here he is again with my piercing between those gold teeth.

"Oh Richard! Damn baby, I'm Cumming!" "Oh shit baby I love you!"

"Not yet JaLisa you don't love me yet if you did you wouldn't give me so much grief."

He releases my clit and has my fluids all over his lips. I grab his face and lick them until they are clean. Now my legs are wrapped around him as he carries me to the bedroom.

"I love you, I whisper in his ear."

"Not yet . . ."

He slams me on the king size and I scoot all the way to the top. Richard grabs me by both of my things and slides me back to the bottom of the bed while he kneels to the floor.

"Oh God! I can't take no more!"

"Yes you can, it's mind over matter."

He is eating me like a wild animal and I swear I can't take no more. I am cumin again and it's happening back to back. My legs are shaking uncontrollably and my body is exhausted.

"Oh Shit!"

"Oh Shit baby!"

"Damn Richard I . . . I can't take no more!" He releases my clit and I slide back to the top of the bed. I am soaking wet I have fluids running all up my ass. He flips me over and I'm on my knees I am so weak right now not only is Richard working his magic but the Vodka has gone to my head.

"Oh Shit!"

It's all I can say as he enters me from behind. He is stroking the shit out of me and "Oh!" it feels so good. I love him. I know I have to love him it just dawned on me that he didn't put on a condom and I'm not on the pill. "Oh!" it feels so good. He flips me in another position. Now I'm on my side with one knee on Richard's chest. How could he be so young and so damn big? I've never had a d--- in me this size. And I love every moment of it. I've been with men much older than him that could never make me feel like this.

I roll over and look at the clock, "Got Dammit Richard I forgot to set the alarm!"

"It's only 7 o'clock, chill."

"Chill I have to be at work by 8 o'clock!"

"Don't worry I'll take you and since it's two of us we can ride the HOV lane."

I'm completely nude and so is he. When I stand to look for my towel his fluids run down my leg. He didn't put on a condom last night. What if I get pregnant? I can't think about that right now its 7:05am and time is just ticking. I jump in the shower and I'm out in two minutes. I grab the first thing I see that doesn't need to be ironed. It's freezing in here so it must be cold outside. I have never been in Miami and felt this cold. I grabbed a sweater and a pair of leggings and slide on my boots on the way out the door. Richard's already warming up the car. The clock reads 7:17 and I am trying to come up with an excuse as to why I'm going to be late again. I swear I am so irresponsible when it comes to Richard first late to class, then no condom last night, now late for work what's next?

The clock on his dash board reads 7:58am as I jump out the car.

"You need lunch money?" Without waiting for a response he shoves about twenty dollars of balled up money in my hand. I can't fuss I don't have time.

"Thanks Richard I love you."

"Not yet JaLisa," he says as he reverses out of the parking lot.

Why the hell does he keep telling me I don't love him? I hop on the first open elevator and it goes to the basement. "That's just my luck!"

I pound on the buttons to go to the second floor and the elevator stalls. It opens at the second floor and guess who I bump into? It's my manager and she does not look happy.

"Hi . . . Good morning I have to go punch in. Sorry."

In an elevated tone she yells at my back:

"When I come from this meeting we need to talk!"

"What the f--- for." I mumble under my breath.

If she heard me she would most likely smack the taste out of my mouth. Bolting through the office to grab the phone on my desk I bump into one of my coworkers.

"Damn JaLisa what the Hell is wrong with you?"

"Look I'm running late I have to punch in."

We have a new time system where we have to punch in from our desk, just another way they have to track our every move. The automated voice says, "The time is now 8:04am please enter your employee number. "Okay so I'm not that late but I wonder what the Hell she wants to talk to me about I ain't done shit, she always want to discuss some shit.

I turn on my computer and open all the icons on my desktop that pertains to my day. Email is the first and my manager has already sent me a message first thing in the morning.

From: Hicks, Brenda
To: Wright, JaLisa
Time: 7:59AM

Subject: We Need To Discuss Some Issues

Good Morning JaLisa:

   I thought I was going to get the opportunity to discuss some issues with you before I headed out to my quarterly meeting but since you are not in yet it will have to wait. I would like to start out by telling you that we are on target with our budget but there are some issues that I wish to go over with you so please prepare to meet with me at noon by then I will be back from my meeting.

                                        Thank you,
                                        Brenda Hicks

   You know what I am not in the mood for this shit today. My feet are already hurting from these boots, I have a ton of work on my desk and I have a paper to write for class by Friday which I had planned to sit here and do while I was working. It's already 8:30am and I haven't gotten one thing accomplished. My cell phone vibrates and the number reads 305-300 . . . It's my mother.
   "What's up Ma? You know I'm at work I'm not supposed to be on this cell phone let me call you from my desk." Click.
   I give her a minute to hang up her phone before I call her back because I know she is just holding it and looking at the receiver right now.
   "Yes, Ma" I'm so irritated right now.
   "When are you going to come by and clean out this stuff in your old room? Since you are in your own place now, I want to turn your room into my sewing room."
   "What! Ma, you called me this early for that?"
   "Yes, JaLisa I know you are not going to move back here especially with your new boyfriend in the picture and all."
   "Ma what does Richard have to do with me coming and cleaning out my old room?" "What do you have against Richard anyway?"

"Look JaLisa I just don't think you should be with anyone that is six years younger that you. What could he possibly have to offer you?" "And those damn gold teeth only drug dealers and rappers have gold teeth!"

"Ma!"

"Don't Ma me listen I'm not telling you how to run your life all I'm saying is how is he going to go on an interview with them teeth in his mouth and they're not even the ones you can just take out!"

"Look Ma I am 28 years old and can date who I damn well please!"

"Girl I will come through this phone and slap you into next week. Remember I brought you in this world and will take you out!"

"Okay Ma, calm down you are right I have no right disrespecting you all I am saying is that you have to get to know Richard he is really sweet and he really cares about me. I know you want the best for me but I love him."

"Love, JaLisa what could you possibly know about love my dear?" "When has love ever paid bills?"

"Ma Richard gives me money all the time."

"And just where does he get this money he doesn't work?"

"Ma I told you he signed a deal with Something Else Music three months ago and they gave him an advancement to complete his album by June of next year."

"JaLisa honey, I gave birth to you I know when something ain't right if you think I believe that lame ass shit. Something is wrong with you! Have you heard any songs from this so called album?"

"Well . . . yeah I heard two, look Ma I will be over there on Saturday to clean out the room for you I have a paper due on Friday so I'm going to be busy till then."

"Look JaLisa I love you and just want . . ."

"I know Ma you just want the best for me we've been over this a million times look I've got to go the boss lady wants to meet with me at noon and I have a lot to do before then. I love you we'll talk later I know you're not finished and I promise I'll be over on Saturday after my Sociology class."

Before she can say anything else my cell is vibrating again. "I gotta go mom." Click.

Another text from Richard *I HAVE A SURPRISE 4 U!*

I type back *WHAT!*

U HAVE 2 CUM 2 MY PLACE 2 GET IT!

I'm smiling from ear to ear I love surprises. I pick back up the phone on my desk and dial his cell.

"What's up baby what you got planned?"

"You will have to wait till you get off work JaLisa."

"See!"

"No really, catch the rail to North side and I'll pick you up from there at 6 o'clock."

"Okay I love you."

"Not yet but you will."

I hung up because I have to get some work done before the boss lady gets back the first thing she is going to ask is what I have been working on.

Noon comes way too fast and she is back at 11:59.

"Damn!"

She goes straight to her office and I swear before she can even sit down she intercoms me. I know who it is but I love to be an ass so I answer.

"Good afternoon thank you for calling TLC Incorporated this is JaLisa Wright speaking how my I help you?"

"JaLisa did you get my email?"

"Yes, Brenda would you like to meet with me now?"

"Yes!" Click.

Okay I need to get this stupid ass smirk off my face before I go up in there. Her office is right next to mine so it only takes a second for me to be standing at her door. I bring my notepad and pen to take notes on whatever it is she wants to discuss.

"Come in JaLisa and close the door behind you."

She doesn't want any witnesses when she sticks her claws in me and draw blood. I shut the door and take a seat as instructed.

"Look JaLisa as I said in the email we are on target and meeting our budget but that is not the only thing in running a successful team."

I'm puzzled, I thought that being on target and meeting budget were the essential tools in running a successful team.

"You JaLisa have way too many personal phone calls and it's been reported that you have even been receiving calls on your cell phone which is against company policy."

I immediately looked at her desk she had two cell phones laid on top of her briefcase.

"Also your attitude over the last few weeks has been intolerable for example, when I was talking to your back this morning."

"But I had to clock in . . ."

"Please don't interrupt. I have also noticed that you are constantly on the internet which is also in the policy manual."

"But, Brenda!"

"Again you are interrupting me. I will give you a chance once I'm finished. All I am trying to tell you is that the Director Mrs. Botch is watching me closely to watch you closely to make sure we are being consistent, she seems to think I allow you to get away with way too much. Do you understand what I am saying?"

"Yes, Brenda I understand."

"Look JaLisa we are the only two black women in this office besides Shelia and she's been here over twenty years so you know they are not going to mess with her. This is what I'm trying to tell you if you want to be promoted you are going to have to make me shine and right now all everyone is looking at is your nasty attitude which is not going to get you anywhere. Do I make myself clear?"

"Yes, Brenda I hear you loud and clear."

"Also one last thing, that boyfriend of yours with the gold teeth I hope you are not bringing him to the Christmas Party."

"Excuse me?"

"I just don't think it would be appropriate I've seen him pick you up and drop you off a few times and well you already know how they view us."

"Look Brenda you can tell me about my work and the personal calls and even the internet but I be damned if I'm going to stand here and let you insult my man. He has done nothing to you and further more, I would not be caught at that tired ass Christmas Party if I was getting paid time and a half to attend with these fake ass people and you . . . You know what? I'm going to leave it at that do you mind if I get back to work I have plenty to do remember we need to stay on target!"

"No, you may not please sit back down. I have put everything we discussed into a written warning and I need you to sign it."

"What! So you are writing me up?"

"Lower your voice JaLisa and please sit back down, Mrs. Botch thought it would be best if we kept track of our conversations."

"Well I tell you what, you tell Mrs. Botch to shove that write-up, up her . . . !"

"JaLisa look I am only trying to help you!"

"Only trying to help me looks to me like you are only trying to get rid of me!"

"You know what, okay you don't have to sign you have every right not to sign but that does not look good. I also need to give you another report to work on and you need to learn to multitask."

I took the report and signed the write up reluctantly. I'm not going to be at this job until I retire and as soon as I get my degree I am out of here. I don't believe I'm being treated fairly. What happened to equal rights? Shit, my Mama is tripping, Brenda tripping and Mrs. Botch is just evil. I need to keep cool because they are paying for me to go to school but that doesn't give them the right to dump all their shit on me. It's totally not fair. I called Brenda on the intercom as soon as I got back to my desk.

"I'm taking an hour for lunch and I'm leaving right now!"

"Look JaLisa I didn't mean to upset you but . . ."

"No need to explain you're the boss I'll be back in an hour!" Click.

At 6 o'clock Richard was waiting for me at North side when I got off the rail. He was standing outside the car and opened the door for me to get in. When he got back in the car I had the seat laid back with my sunglasses on. I cried the entire ride home. Today was not a good day for me and I just want to go home and crawl under the bed that's how low I feel. But Richard has other plans he just drove to his apartment on 27th Avenue. I really don't like coming over here after dark but I'm not about to put up a fight this evening. We walk into his place and he has a path of rose pedals from the front door to the bathroom and the lights are dim.

"How did you get the light to dim?"

"Just take off those boots so that you can feel the petals against your feet."

He undressed me and led me to the bathroom where he had the tub filled with bubbles. I stuck my toe in because I thought it would be cold.

"I filled it with all hot water before I left out to pick you up so it's had time to cool off."

I sunk down in the tub and tears ran down my face.

"You didn't have to do this."

"Yes I did there's more I just want you to relax first."

He proceeded to wash me up. He took a wash cloth and lathered it with soap and washed around my neck and ears.

"Lift up."

I did as he gently washed my back. He lifted my arms and washed them and moved down to my breasts. By then both my nipples were erect. I just laid back and let him wash all the stress off my body. He let some of the water out and added more hot water just the way I like it. As the water was going out he used that opportunity to wash my inner thighs and my clit. He lifted my clit ring to make sure it was clean and as he touched it I felt a sensation radiate up my spine. I let out a soft moan. He took the wash cloth and ran it over each leg and lastly my feet.

"Stay here and relax a moment I'll be back to get you."

I didn't even respond I'm just laying here reflecting on my day. Mama pissed me off, then Brenda, but laying here nothing even matters. I keep telling Richard that I love him and he keeps responding with not yet and he's right I love what he does for my body. This young man sure has experience in pleasing women. He interrupts my thoughts when he's back so soon to get me out of the bath. When he opens the door I smell something very nice it smells like a restaurant. He pulls the plug out the tub and rinses the remainder of bubbles from my thighs and ass.

"What's that smell?"

"I made us some dinner."

He opens a huge towel like one you would take to the beach and dries me off the rose petals are sticking to the bottom of my feet feeling like silk. I follow him to the room and one of my teddies is laid across the bed. I remember I left it over here a few weeks ago and he's washed it for me. It smells so good. He has his robe laid out on the bed next to my teddy so I put that on also.

He has a little table in the dining room that seats four and has it set for me and him. Tonight we are eating Stouffers Lasagna the kind that you can either stick in the oven or microwave.

"This is really delicious Richard and the bath took the stress off that I had been carrying around all day."

"That's cool JaLisa I brought you over to my place and have done these things because I need to talk to you about some things."

"Okay then let's talk."

"Well the first thing I wanted to tell you is that I've completed all that I can do for the songs that I am contributing to the record that Something Else Music has me working on. It's a variety album that three other artists and myself are on and what I'm trying to tell you is that I will be leaving for New York in one week so that my songs can be mixed. Remember when I told you that they gave me a check?"

"Yes, I remember."

"Okay let me explain there are a series of checks with the contract that I signed the first was for ten thousand dollars and that covers just me doing the portion that I have completed thus far."

"Okay go on I'm listening."

"The second check will be for fifty thousand and that portion covers me spending time in New York and doing some radio advertisements that I have been asked to do. Now the catch is to continue receiving checks I am going to have to go on tour with the other artist to promote the album and I need to know are you going to be okay with that. I want to know that you have my back and you will be here for me when I get back home."

"Baby you have to trust that I will have your back. While you are away I am just going to focus on my school work and my job because they are trying to get rid of me."

"Well when I get back if you want to quit we can talk about that."

"Baby I can't quit my job they are paying for me to go to school and all I want right now is my degree."

"Looks like for now I will be away for about three weeks so what is my baby going to do for sex. I know you love to have sex.

I may have to buy you some toys."

"Yeah you do . . . that way we can go pick them out together."

Tonight Richard and I are not making love we've just decided to spend time holding each other. I really know that he cares about me and three weeks ain't that long to wait for him to come home and tear this p---- up. Maybe we need a break anyway so that I can refocus. When he finally fell asleep I slipped out the bed and opened his lap top. He told me that this was a good deal that he found at a Pawn Shop not too far from the 183rd flea market. For his screen saver he has my name in big bubble letters. That is so sweet. I'm not even going to go through any of his files because as they say when you look for trouble you find it. It takes me about an hour and a half to finish my paper for Sociology class and now I'm ready to finally get some sleep. I've set the alarm on my cell phone to go off at 6 o'clock so that Richard can run me past my house in the morning to get clothes for work.

When I finished my paper I saved it to a disk that I had in my purse then slid in bed with Richard. I push my body as close to him as I can get and he's now hard as a rock. "Ummm." Taking my hand behind me I stroke him through his boxer shorts. I know he's half sleep so I slide under the covers and take his manhood in my mouth. Yeah, he's awake now. He's running his fingers though my braids as he says with sleep in his voice "Damn baby that feels right."

"Shh, let me do this."

He's not circumcised so there's extra skin that I have to play with. I roll my tongue around the head and his body stiffens. With my mouth full I tell him "I can taste your pre-cum."

Richard loves when I go down on him because it's not often that I give him this special treat. It's after midnight and I know that I need to get some rest but all I can think about is that he's going to be in New York alone with all them hot ass girls. Especially with him going on tour there are always the groupie bitches. When I look up at Richard his eyes are rolled in the back of his head his body relaxes and my mouth fills. I've got enough protein to last me until the next time I decide to give him a treat. When I finally come up to where he's lying, he wraps his arms around me and pulls me close to him and kisses my ears and sucks on my neck. I'm beginning to get moist as he pulls my body even closer. He has me on my side and enters me from behind. He's still erect even though he just released himself. I push my ass back as far as it can go and he slides his hands down to my waist.

"Oh Richard" I moan.

My body is releasing fluids and I feel myself cumin "Oh, Richard, yes baby, right there!"

I love the way he is stroking me from behind. He is by far the best lover I've ever had. Richard makes my body explode from the inside out. I don't know what I'm going to do about hormones while he is away. I'm definitely going to have to invest in some toys like he suggested. His rhythm picks up as his body thrusts against mine. He penetrates me over and over until finally he releases.

"Oh! JaLisa!"

I take a deep breath and doze off to sleep.

~ RICHARD ~

You know I really do care about JaLisa she tells me all the time that I am a woman pleaser but to tell you the truth she is the first woman that I've ever had. All the rest have been girls that I have had to teach them what I like but not with JaLisa she knows how to please me. I respect her to the utmost cause she's holding it down. She has no kids, has her own crib and her own job not to mention that she's in school. That tells me right there that she wants to better herself and I'm all for any woman trying to better themselves. That's like when I told her about the music thing she ain't trying to sweat me for my change I actually have to force her to take money from me. Sometimes I just put the money in her purse while she's asleep or if she's getting out the car I'll shove it in her hand and pull off.

She's so pretty with her rich brown skin tone and when the sun or light shines on her eyes they almost look hazel. I've been thinking that when I go up to New York I'm going to be faithful I know it's going to be chicks all over the place with the tour and all but those bitches ain't gonna have *nothing* on my baby.

~ JaLisa ~

Richard left in a week as he had planned. He had me drive him to Ft. Lauderdale Airport for his flight to New York. We never made it to get the toys and I didn't make it over Mama's to clean out the room either. I told her that since Richard was going away I would have plenty of time to get over to my old room and that maybe I may even spend a few days with her. She liked the sound of that and left me alone about it. Richard made love to me very well several times before he left just to make sure I don't step out on him. He decided to leave me his car. Now I can take care of a lot of things that I have been slacking on. When I took him to the airport we shared an embrace and a kiss so juicy he said he was tempted to cancel his trip and go back home with me. As I'm walking out of the terminal he tells me to look in the glove box when I get to the car and to make sure I remove the white envelope inside. When I walk back to the car my eyes are filled with tears I am really going to miss him. I have gotten so used to him being around. I get to the car and the glove box is locked but the key to the ignition opens it and inside lays a white envelope with a card inside. I open the card with out reading it and there are twenty $100.00 bills inside. Tears flood my eyes as I read the card.

> *"I don't want my woman to want for a thing! When I come back home there's gonna be so much more of this. JaLisa you mean the world to me and I want you to spoil yourself while I'm away. Go get your nails done, a massage, new clothes and new shoes whatever that you think will put a smile on that pretty face of yours."*

> *Richard*

P.S. Keep It Tight A'aight!

I have to get myself together before I can even pull off. When I pull up to the parking attendant to exit the garage I hand the girl inside a crisp $100.00 bill she looks at it, hold it to the sun and say "This the smallest thing you got it is only $2.00 to park here!"

"Yes that's all I have not unless you want my parking to be free today!"

"I don't think so!" she says as she snaps her neck.

"Well I guess you better give me change then."

The yellow pole lifts and I call Mama. She answers on the third ring. "Hello."

"Mama are you dressed I wanna come take you out?"

"Yeah I'm dressed just came back from Winn Dixie they got a serious sell on can goods. I Got me an entire case for just $5.00."

"Okay Mama I'm on my way we gon hang out for a while so bring some comfortable shoes."

"How are you getting here? Where are you at now?"

"I have Richard's car and I'm leaving Ft. Lauderdale Airport I'll be there in about twenty minutes."

"Okay." Click

It's only gonna take me about fifteen minutes the way I'm driving. My Mama lives in Opa Locka on the good side of the rail road tracks she's been living in the same house since I was 3 years old. Twenty-five years in the same house. When my daddy died I was sixteen years old and a senior in High School it hurt Mama so bad but she held it together. Daddy died from a bad heart and I believe he knew to expect the worst after he had his surgery earlier that year because he took out an insurance policy that would leave Mama enough money to pay off the house and have back up for the bills. She never told me how much he left her but any time I need something she's always there for me. So, I pull into Mama's driveway and park behind her Cadillac and she's standing behind the screen door just looking at me. When I get out the car she opens the screen for me to come in.

"Ma you know its Richards car I just dropped him off at the Airport he's in New York for three weeks doing the music thing. Come on let's go I want to take you out for a while you deserve it."

Mama didn't put up a fight she grabbed her jacket and locked the door and followed me to the car. I opened the door for her and helped her inside not that she needed any help but I just wanted to give her some extra attention.

We drove to 57th Avenue a nail shop called "Miami Nails" where Mama and I both got pedicures and manicures. Mama doesn't like acrylic overlays so neither of bothered to get those. The Korean women here are always so friendly. We didn't do much talking when it was time to get pedicures the only two booths left were separate and I liked that even better I knew Mama was full of questions yet to be asked. I paid the lady at the register as we left and gave a $10.00 tip. Mama was looking at me funny cause she knows I'm usually tight on money. Three dollars is the most I usually ever give for a tip. When we go to the car she said, "What's up JaLisa tell me what's going on?"

I just shrugged my shoulders and drove to the Chili's across the street because this is one of Mama's favorite restaurants. She loves the way they make their Margarita's. Before we get out of the car I say to her "look Mama it ain't nothing wrong with me wanting to spend the day with you and spoil you a little. I'm always either working or going to school or with Richard lately and we hardly ever spend any quality time together so just let me do this okay Mama."

"Okay dear it's just I know you have bills . . ."

"Mama please let me do this I've been saving a little something."

Now I know she ain't buying the saving bit at all. If anything my Mama knows I can't save the pennies in my water jug for too long before wrapping them and using them for something. She's enjoying the attention so she's going along with it. When we get into the Chili's Mama requests the corner booth she can't stand for a lot of traffic while she gets her eat on. Our waitress is quick and on her toes this afternoon. Mama orders a Margarita and the Bar-B-Que rib special while I order the lemon pepper salmon; a loaded baked potato with a Caesar salad heavy on the ranch.

I didn't order anything to drink for myself just a Root Beer cause I know she would be looking at me side ways especially since I have to drive home. Before our food came Mama reached across the table and held both my hands.

"JaLisa I am so proud of you. You have really grown up to be a beautiful young woman and you are on the path to success. I just want you to keep at it and I'd like to apologize for butting in about you and Richard I just don't want to see you hurt."

"I know Mama there is no need to apologize; you're always going to voice your opinion and I wouldn't expect anything less."

The waitress came with our drinks and Mama sipped as if she were savoring every salty moment.

"You know baby I don't get out that often and this feels really good."

"Good I'm glad you're enjoying yourself."

It didn't take long for our food to come and we both ate like we hadn't eaten all day. When it was time for the check Mama offered to help pay but I gave her the "don't go there" look and she withdrew her hand from her purse. After two Margarita's Mama was buzzed I could tell by the glassy look in her eyes. I wasn't finished yet once we finished at Chili's I drove Mama down to her favorite store "Target". I needed to pick up another Glade Plug In was what I told her to get her to come inside. We went from isle to isle checking out good buys. She was eyeing a Crystal candle set so I picked it up and put it in the cart. We found my Plug In and got a few more things before we headed back to Mama's. I was very conscious of my driving because Mama is temperamental when it comes to being escorted around. She really hasn't let any one drive her around since Daddy. She's been so independent.

I was going to stay the night at Mama's but decided against it cause I know at the crack of dawn she was gonna have me up cleaning out my old room and I'm not in the mood for any early Sunday rise. I have to be at work bright and early Monday morning so I'm going to enjoy one day of rest. I kissed her on the forehead and headed back to my place. On the way home I stop at "Willie's Liquor's" on 183rd and 42nd Avenue to pick up a bottle of Vodka and grapefruit juice. When I finally made it to my place I walked in and the first thing I notice is my answering machine light on. I pick up the receiver and dial my pass code. "You have one message." It's from Richard.

"Hello my beautiful black princess I just wanted to let you know that I've landed safely. I'm staying at the J.W. Marriott on 5th Avenue, Suite 1222. The room is great but it's cold as shit up here I called the house instead of calling your cell cause a nigga hoping that you're out doing something special for yourself. Call me when you get a chance either on the cell or at the hotel. The number is 212-423 . . ." Click

Before I called Richard back I wanted to totally unwind so I pour myself a drink and ran a bubble bath. With my Love Spell in hand I light two of the candles that I bought from "Target" today. I step into the tub and dial Richard's cell with my dry hand. He answers on the second ring.

"Hey love, why are you not out still spoiling yourself?"

"Mama and I went out for a girls day and I'm just getting back in."

"Is that bath water I hear?"

"Yes baby I'm calling you from the bath tub I miss you already."

I take the hand I'm not holding the phone with and rub it over my clit. Richard hears the change in my voice and asks

"What are you doing?"

"Just rubbing myself, that's all."

"I knew you were doing something because your tone changed."

"So how's New York?"

"Well its cold but what can you expect, two weeks before Christmas?"

"Damn baby I didn't even think about you not being here for Christmas."

"Yeah me neither it dawned on me on the way here. New York is really lit up this time of year. They go all out up here not like Miami at all."

"So what do you have planned for tonight in the city that never sleeps?"

"Not much, since they have all the artists staying in the same hotel we were thinking about meeting up at the bar. I'm not planning to stay too late we have an early rise to be at WJNY Radio Station at 7am and it's gonna takes us about a half hour to get there."

"You can handle it, you're use to getting up with me early."

There's a knock at his door. It's one of the other artists, they are heading down to the bar now.

"I'll call you when I get back in if it's not too late. I know how you hate to have your sleep interrupted in the middle of the night."

"Okay baby talk to you later."

~ RICHARD ~

JT knocked on the door while I was on the phone with JaLisa so I told her I would call her back. When we got down stairs to the bar Raymond and Lil Mike were already there with drinks in hand. I can already tell that this is going to be an interesting trip. Word got out that it was us that signed with Something Else Music and women have been swarming these dudes like bees to honey. JT already done slipped up and said "What your girl doesn't know won't hurt her." And I had to tell him about that shit. "First of all I'm not dealing wit no girl. I have a woman back home and let's leave it at that."

I can tell these nigga's some hoes but I ain't trying to get down like that. I have some good shit going on and I ain't trying to wreck my shit for no one night stands. The music here is jacked up until they played some of Terrible T's new shit. They're playing this cut with Linkin Park that ain't to be messed wit. JaLisa had my d--- rock hard with that bathtub shit. She knows exactly what she be doing to get me right in the palm of her hand. If that nigga JT hadn't knocked on my door I'd be beatin my shit right now. Lil Mike and Raymond done hooked up wit some hoes already and on they way back to their rooms.

JT says, "Yo next round on me what you havin?"

"I'll take another Heineken thanks man."

"Those hoes gon be the down fall of those two dudes I hope they be ready when it's time to roll in the morning cause I ain't being late for no one when my money is on the line."

"I know that's right!" I said nodding my head. Shit I ain't trying to mess up my money either after this next Heineken I'm heading in so I can be straight for my first interview."

"That lil shorty checkin you out I know you got a woman but man she fine as shit."

"Nah man you got it won't you try to holla at that?"

"Yo she all up in your shit not mine."

Just as he said that she walks this way and I've got to admit she has a phat ass. Got damn she looks like one of dem model chicks. I act like I don't even see her ass coming.

"Hi my name is Monica I was watching you since you came in, y'all two here alone?"

"Hey Monica what up? Yeah, we alone but I was just about to leave."

"No don't leave yet the night is just getting started my girl Resha and I wanted to come over for drinks."

JT says, "Resha who is Resha and where she at?"

"She went to the ladies room to check her make up."

JT turns to me and says, "Hey man one more drink won't hurt and you ain't payin it's on me so have another."

"Man I don't know I ain't trying to be down here all night with these . . ."

Resha cut me off when she came and sat beside JT his attention was totally on her. Looks like she had a boob job cause her titties sittin up so high on her chest looks like they about to pop out that tight ass shirt she wearing.

Monica says to me "that's Resha we're here for two weeks from Atlanta doing these seminars for the Law firm that we work for. Actually it's the lawyers that we work for that are in the seminars all we do is set up the rooms. We hand out pamphlets, coordinate the events and take notes . . . Sorry look at me I'm just going on and on about my boring shit . . . I do love New York thought it's just cold up here compared to Atlanta. Where are you from?"

"Miami."

"Oh yeah I was down there this past summer for Memorial Day weekend it was packed with nigga's down on South Beach. Do you live near there?"

"Yeah bout twenty minutes."

"That is so cool it is so beautiful there on the beach. Before I went down there I had never seen blue water before. We don't have blue water in Atlanta."

"Oh yeah."

"So what you doing up here?" Monica asked.

"I'm working on this music thing."

"Wow! What do you do? Sing, rap, freestyle what?"

"Actually . . ."

JT interrupts when he says, "We'll be back we bout to hit the dance floor."

He must have noticed the disturbed look on my face so he slapped me on my shoulder. He sure looks cozy with Resha and I know he don had at least three drinks. He dun got him one but I ain't going out like that.

Monica asks "Do you want to dance Richard?"

It was something about the way she said my name. She made me lose my train of thought.

"Nah . . . I gotta be up early in the morning I'm done I'mma head back to my room it's already midnight and I need to get some Z's."

"Okay but don't leave me here alone what floor are you on?"

"Twelfth floor."

"Me too, Suite 1211."

"I'm in 1222."

We walked out together and took the elevator to the 12th floor. She keeps looking at me and licking her lips but I can't go there. We are down the hall and we got to her room first.

"It was such a pleasure meeting you Richard I hope this isn't our last time seeing each other. I'm here for two more weeks so I know I'll run into you again."

"Nice meeting you too Monica you pretty cool."

I started to walk away and she said, "Richard wait . . . would you like to come in?"

"Nah I have to . . ."

"I know you have to get up early but I don't wanna be alone tonight and since you're alone I was just wondering if we could . . ."

"Look Monica maybe if this was another time but I have a . . ."

"I kind of already figured that you have a girl. We don't have to sleep together I just . . . well I don't know but I'm really feeling you I just feel like I can talk to you about anything . . . okay I don't want to ruin it thanks for having a drink with me . . . good night Richard."

"Good night Monica" was all I could say as I watched her walk into her room and close the door she really wanted me to come in but I can't be caught slippin. She seems like a really nice girl. Damn I look down and my d--- is hard as shit I wonder did she notice that shit. As I head to my room I hear JT and Resha in the hall they both go to his room and close the door behind them. When I get inside my room I close the door and close my eyes, "Man, I miss JaLisa I don't know if I can take three weeks of this shit!"

I turn on the hot water to the shower and the steam instantly fills the bathroom. It's something about hotel showers that feel so damn good. I'm just standing here letting the hot water beat on my back. I want to call JaLisa but it's too late I'll call her after the interview. I take my d--- in my hand and my mind goes from JaLisa's beautiful lips to Monica's phat ass. Damn why am I sitting here holding my d--- thinking about that chick? I step out of the shower and I can hear the phone next to my bed ringing. I trip over my pants that I left in the middle of the floor so I'm out of breath when I answer. It may be JaLisa calling.

"Hello . . . JaLisa?"

"So that's her name?"

"What? Who is this?"

"I'm sorry this is Monica I called down stairs and they put me through to your room you said you were in 1222. Look I didn't mean to bother you it's just Resha hasn't gotten in yet and I know she's with JT. Do you know his room number? I need to tell her that one of the lawyers called while we were out, and said that we need to set up an hour earlier tomorrow because they have a special guest coming."

"Yeah . . . wait I think he's in 1215 if not try 1217."

"So what were you doing did I disturb anything you sounded out of breath?"

"Yeah I was taking a shower and I uh tripped over my pants when I heard the phone ringing I thought you were . . ."

"I know you thought I was your girl you sound like you miss her."

"Yeah."

"Sorry again for bothering you."

"Nah it's all good I'm about to get some sleep."

"Okay see you tomorrow."

~ JALISA ~

It felt strange going to bed alone last night I'm so used to Richard being here or me being at his place things just didn't feel the same. I lay in this big ole bed of mine and rubbed on myself until I fell asleep. I waited for Richard to call when he came back from the bar but I guess it was too late when he got in. Mama called me first thing this morning to thank me for taking her out yesterday. It makes me feel so good to know that I put a smile on her face. I keep thinking about the fact that Richard is not gonna be here for Christmas. I would love to pay him a surprise visit but I know Mama don't want to be alone either and if I went to surprise Richard this would be the first Christmas that we weren't together. Mama just wouldn't understand me leaving her here alone on Christmas to be with Richard. I finally got out of bed and did a few loads of laundry while the last was drying I dumped out my purse to clean it out. I have $1,800.00 left of the money that Richard gave me so I took $1,000.00 and put it in the back of my closet in one of my old shoeboxes for safe keeping. No sense in me putting it in the bank, I would not be able to get to it fast enough. My cell phone rings and its Jasmine one of the only friends I still keep in contact with from high school.

"Hey J what's up?"

"Girl you ain't gon believe this shit!"

"What! Is everything okay?"

"Hell yeah shit is tight girl I've been going out with this dude name Rashod from The Radio station. He hooked me up with front row seats to see Terrible T in concert and you know that if Terrible T is here that Miz Thang' is gonna be here too."

"Is that the concert that R. Mann was supposed to be doing with him?"

"Yeah girl but it's a lot of shit behind that I asked Rashod but he said that R. Mann is his boy so he don't wanna go into it."

"Damn J that's tight I'm happy for you. I hope you have a great time."

"Bitch didn't I say he got me front row seats!"

"So?"

"So, that means we are going to see Terrible T tonight!"

"J you are shitting me. You know how much I love that nigga Terrible T!"

"I'm about to ride out to Aventura Mall to see if I can find me some new shoes."

"Cool I'm wit that how about this I can come and pick you up?"

"When you get a ride you ain't tell me about a new car?"

"Nah Richard left me his car and girl he left me money too so I'll be there in about a half hour."

"Cool that will give me enough time I'll be waiting down stairs."

~ RICHARD ~

T he boys and I made it to the station on time for the interview. The interview went so well they really made us look good, they gave all the tour dates and locations and this station has about one million listeners. We all rode together in a Cadillac Truck that Something Else Music provided for us the driver is this huge dude that knows the city well. We went down all back streets a few alleys and ended up in an underground garage that has an elevator that led right up to the station. JT and I sat in the back with Raymond. JT kept shaking his head and smiling he said "Man we need to talk." Resha must have put it on him last night cause this nigga got a Kool-Aid grin this morning. So when we get back to the hotel Lil Mike and Raymond went shopping and JT and I sat down stairs at the bar and ordered club sandwiches with fries.

"Yo that shorty Resha put it on your ole boy last night you dig."

"I figured that by that Kool-Aid grin you had all morning."

"So what happened with you and Monica?"

"Ain't shit man I'm being faithful, JaLisa would kick my black ass."

"Yo I had Resha screaming a nigga's name last night. I invited her to the first show tomorrow."

"What, you got to be jokin! So that means Monica is gonna be in the front row of our first show?"

"Is that a problem? Don't tell me you sweet on Monica?"

"Nah man it ain't a problem."

I rolled out on JT I don't know how to feel about that shit he did. Tomorrow is our first show and he pulls a stunt like this. I know I said that shit ain't a problem but that puts pressure on a nigga. I need to talk to JaLisa so I dial her cell. She picks up and I can hear her friend Jasmine

28

in the background running her lips. I don't really care for Jasmine cause she's always runnin game on nigga's and I think she's a bad influence on JaLisa.

"What's up baby what you doing."

"Jasmine and I are on our way to Aventura Mall."

"That's cool you gon buy you something nice?"

"Yeah baby something cute Jasmine lucked up and got us tickets to go see Terrible T. tonight at the American Airline Arena."

"That's tight I know how you love Terrible T. you just be safe cause dem lil Mama's down there gon be going bananas."

"I know baby I will. I miss you so much. How did the interview go?"

"It was all good they did a good spot light on us."

"Hold on baby I'm trying to park the car we just pulled up to the mall."

"Just holla back baby tear the mall up."

"I miss you Richard."

"I miss you too baby."

JaLisa's occupied and I'm about to lose my mind. This is only my second day here and I feel like I'm about to bust. Just as I was about to take a shower to relieve my mind someone knocks on the door. When I open the door my heart is bout to jump through my throat.

"Monica what are you doing here?"

"Resha and I ran into JT downstairs and he said I could find you here."

"Oh he did, did he?"

"You care for some company I brought us some drinks?"

She was carrying a bag with a bottle of Remy Martin and a two liter Coke. I have a feeling I'm going to regret this later but I really don't feel like being alone. Monica invites herself in walking right past me and plopping down on the bed. When I watched her walk passed me I felt a chill run through me. She's wearing this tight ass long black skirt with a baby blue sweater. Baby blue's my favorite color and I can't take my eyes off the way it hugs her breasts.

"How old are you Richard?"

"Twenty-two and you"

"Me too we have something in common I thought you were much older that me."

"Why would you say that?"

"Cause you are so mature."

As I was walking around the room she asked me to make her a drink. "I don't have any ice."

"I don't need ice the Coke is already cold and ice only waters down the Remy anyway."

I made drinks for Monica and myself and turned on the TV to break the silence. We watched E! *True Hollywood Stories* for about fifteen minutes before Monica finally said, "Richard do you find me attractive?"

"Hell yeah . . . I mean Monica I think you are beautiful."

"But . . ."

"But . . . What?"

"I know there's a but so let me hear it."

"There's no but . . ."

Before I could get out my sentence Monica had her hand on my leg and kissed me on my lips. I could have stopped there but I didn't she sat on my lap and I slowly kissed her lips. She has on a gloss that tastes sweet like strawberries. She sucked on my bottom lip and my d--- got hard as a rock. She started sucking on my neck and her hand went to the rock. What am I doing? If JaLisa ever found out about this she would trip out! We stopped kissing and I got up and walked over to the window to pour myself another drink this time straight Remy no ice, no chaser. Monica walks over behind me and massages my shoulders as I'm looking out on New York City. All you can see is thousands of lights. From the reflection in the window I watch as Monica take off her sweater. I turn around and she's so close I feel shorty breathing on me. Damn she's hot. I can't stop I take her by the waist and pull her to me. I am so wrong for this shit and I know it. Her body is perfect and her skin is so soft. I'm sucking on her neck and rubbing my hands through all of this long ass hair she has. The shit doesn't even look real but it is.

"Please make love to me Richard." I take my hand and slide it down her skirt inside her thong and she is closely shaved just like I like it. Monica is soaking wet. She's moaning as I rub on her clit. I grab my cup and in one swallow finish off my Remy and it burns my chest. She lifts my T-shirt over my head and throws it over the chair, unbutton my jeans next thing I know she has my back up against the window and she's giving a nigga some crucial head.

"What you doing down there girl?"

She don't even come up for air I just wanna bust all in her mouth. My mind wonders to the last time JaLisa gave me head the night I told her I was going to New York. Before I could release in her mouth I pulled her away and lifted her up off her knees. I don't know what the hell is wrong with me but I don't want to bust in her mouth. I press her body up against the wall and sucked I know at least three hickeys on her neck. When I picked her up she looked me in the eyes and said "Richard please make love to me. I need to feel you right now."

Shit I don't have any condoms I wasn't expecting no shit like this.

"I don't have no . . ."

She reaches on the edge of the bed for her purse fumble around for a minute and pulls out a box of three "Magnum Gold's."

"You came prepared?"

"I knew how bad I wanted you. I just didn't want this to be your excuse."

I reached behind her back and unhooked her bra and her breast are firm and real they just sit up on her chest like a super-models would. I took her nipples in my mouth like a newborn baby ready to be fed. Monica moaned so softly as I slide down both her skirt and her thongs. I couldn't believe myself when I started sucking on her clit. It feels funny not sucking on a pierced clit. Damn I miss JaLisa.

"Oh your mouth is so warm Richard."

This girl is moving like she ain't neva had a nigga lick this clit. Her p---- taste like her lips, strawberries. Damn she tastes sweet. I played with her clit a little.

"Richard!"

Yeah she likes it I proceed to suck on her like it's a mission. Monica is shaking and shit like she's going to convulsions.

"Richard Got Damn Richard!"

As she cums I drink every drop and she tastes like sweet nectar.

When she finally can't take no more I release her clit and ask "Are you straight or do you want the d--- too."

"Richard please give me the d--- I need to feel you."

Her p---- is drippin wet when I put the condom on she pulls me on top of her but before I can put it in she rolls me over and asks, "Can I ride you first?"

She slides my rock hard d--- inside of her and it takes a minute to get in. Shorty feels like a virgin. Her p---- is so tight it feels like the condom is bout to pop. She hops on like a pro once it's in and begins to ride me like her life depended on it.

"Why you so damn tight Monica?"

"I never had a d--- this big and I ain't had none in almost a year. My last boyfriend left me for an older woman and . . . Oh shit you feel good Richard!"

"I don't believe how tight you are! Got damn girl you make a nigga wanna bust off."

She rode me for as long as she would take it and then got on her knees. I took her from the back as she got wetter and wetter. I slid her down to the bottom of the bed and turned her over to her back and stroked the shit out of her before I felt myself cumming. I couldn't hold it any longer. She pulled me into the bathroom with her and we took a shower together. This girl is beautiful and I'm rock hard again. Monica gets on her knees in the shower and wants to give me head but I won't let her. I pull her up and start kissing her it's like she's melting in my arms. Her hair is wet and it's hanging down her back.

"Why won't you let me . . ."

"Because"

"Because what? Don't I make you feel good?"

"Yes that's the problem I'm not supposed to be feeling this way."

"I won't tell your girl if you won't."

"You real funny you know that?"

We dried off and she put on the robe that was hanging in the bathroom. I wrapped up with a towel and we had another drink.

~ JALISA ~

The American Airline Arena is so packed by the time we make it to the ticket booth. It took us at least forty-five minutes to get to the front of the line. I'm so glad I brought some comfortable shoes today at the mall cause Jasmine is complaining already I told this girl not to buy any heels but she insisted. We have our front row tickets and the back stage passes are around our necks. We're seated like twenty minutes before the show begins. The lights in the Arena go dim and the bass goes deafening "Put Em Up . . . Put Em Up!" Terrible T. erupts to the stage and the crowd goes mad wild. I jump to my feet and look over to Jasmine and she's still seated her cell is lighting up and she's receiving a text. "Put Em Up . . . Put Em Up!" She grabs me by my pants until I sit down and shows me the message. *I SEE YA MADE IT! MEET ME IN DA BACK AFTA THE LAST SONG SOUND STAGE ROOM 125! HAV FUN & MAKE SUM NOISE!*

This totally energizes her and she's up on her feet. Terrible T. is calm as he lays down his lyrics there are two dudes on the stage with him and he has a band. Two more songs and he finally broke a sweat. I've never seen anyone perform live and as calm as he is. I guess he doesn't let all of this go to his head. He looks in our direction and I see he looks into my eyes I hold his attention for like five seconds as I lick my lips. Jasmine grabs my arm and screams in my ear. "Did you see him look at you!" I just nod and blush I knew he was looking at me but to have Jasmine see him that is tight. The music plays for *"Me and Mrs. Jones"* and everyone's looking for Miz Thang' to make her entrance. She comes out wearing these killer red bottom pumps and a tight black mini dress. The crowd goes even wilder for Miz Thang' than they did for Terrible T. "Me and she got a thang going on." Terrible T shows more emotion when Miz Thang' comes out. They look so hot standing next to each other. All this excitement and still I miss Richard. I pray he does well at his first show tomorrow. I would love to be in New York supporting him. I wonder what he's doing right now.

~ RICHARD ~

W e had another drink and Monica took off the robe. She said "if this is going to be our last time together I don't want to ever forget it." She pushed me down on the bed and got on her knees.

"Got damn girl yo lips feel like butta."

She was just working her magic and I grabbed her hair. She has a great rhythm I just laid back and let her do her magic shorty got a nigga's toes curling and shit. I can't bust in her mouth so I grab another condom and sit her on top of my d---. She's riding me like a stallion while my legs hang off the side of the bed. She's sitting on me and I swear besides JaLisa, this is some of the best p---- I've ever had. We roll over and go to the top of the bed. Missionary style and she has her feet on the headboard. This is not just good it's great. It takes me a long time to cum because we did it earlier.

~ JASMINE ~

The last song played and Terrible T. was on the stage by himself with the band. He thanks everyone for coming out and for supporting his last album. He said he was gonna leave the stage for the younger cats. It seemed like he looked at me again but that time it just may be me wanting him to look my way. Before the song finished Jasmine and I went to the backstage and found the room. She saw Rashod and jumped in his arms kissing him on his face "thank you Rashod" was all I said.

"How late are y'all gonna be able to stay out?" he asked.

Jasmine said "well I'm out all night but JaLisa has to be to work in the morning."

"Let me speak for myself Jasmine. Rashod I can handle mine what you got planned."

"Terrible T. is having an after party exclusively for radio personalities and their guest at Club Bed in an hour."

Jasmine and I both looked at each other and showed all whites.

I said, "I'm game!"

Jasmine said, "You know I'm game!"

"Okay so y'all meet me there just show your passes at the door and they will let you into VIP I'll beat y'all there."

It took us at least an hour to get there and we couldn't find parking so I let valet park the car. When we got to VIP not only was Rashod there but Terrible T was there without Miz Thang'. It was said that she had to catch a flight to California for a video shoot in the morning. Rashod introduced us to Terrible T. first Jasmine as his boo and me as his boo's best friend.

I said, "Hi Terrible T. you were so great tonight I love seeing you perform live."

36

"Thanks I appreciate that you girls gon stay awhile I have to get wit a few folks and we can have some drinks."

There was already a bottle of Cristal on the table so we started on that.

Jasmine whispers in my ear "girl he actually talked to you."

My brown face turned blood red and I can feel it. I know Terrible T. ain't thinking about me he has this hot ass chick Miz Thang' and who am I?

Rashod says "Yo if he said he's coming back believe me the way he looked you up and down he's coming back."

~ RICHARD ~

I don't have no energy left between this Remy and Monica they don sucked a nigga dry. Monica don passed out so I pulled the covers up to her neck cause she naked. I'm just laying here on my back in the dark. I wonder what JaLisa's doing right now. I can't call her cause if Monica wakes up she may start talking. I know I'm wrong as shit for sleeping wit this girl but what can I do now. She's even beautiful in her sleep. I'm so glad that she lives in Atlanta and I live in Miami cause us being in the same state just wouldn't work. I sure hope JaLisa don't do no shit like this to me. "I f---ed up." I can't even sleep because I want to know if JaLisa is okay. Did she make it home from the show? I can't take it so I grab my cell phone, took it into the bathroom and lock the door behind me. I dial her cell and the call is forwarded to her voicemail.

"Yo JaLisa what's up baby I just wanna know if you made it in okay?"

I hang up and call the house phone and the machine picks up afta three rings.

"Yo baby what's up I wanna know did you make it in?"

~ JASMINE ~

Terrible T. came back to sit with us and him and Rashod were talking about some up and coming events that he was going to be doing here in Miami. He then turned to me and said, "So JaLisa where yo man at?"

"He's in New York."

"Oh yeah and he left you here alone for how long?"

"Three weeks."

"You eva come up to New York?"

"Neva been outta Miami."

"Man you gotta travel and see things Miami is beautiful but there's a whole world out there waiting for you to see it."

"I'm in school now but when I get out maybe I'll travel."

"How about next weekend I'm doing another show in New York and I'd love to see your pretty face when I look out into the audience."

"Are you serious how would I get there? Where would I stay?"

"Being I am who I am I have a hook up on airline tickets and hotel rooms."

Rashod butted in . . . "Yeah JaLisa I'll be there and Jasmine you can come too if you want."

Terrible T. said "I leave here in the morning and I sure don't want this to be our last time seeing each other."

I'm thinking what did I do to have Terrible T. interested in me? Maybe cause I ain't sweatin him. He's not coming on to me or trying to get the ass we are just having a conversation. I really don't believe this shit. I'm totally feeling him but I'm trying to play cool in reality I want to just jump outta my skin. This shit is so unreal. One, I'm sitting on a bed in a club which is not out of the ordinary for Miami but to be sitting on this bed wit Terrible T. He is so much cuter in person then on TV. Jasmine and Rashod left us to go dance and it's just me and him. All I can think of to say is, "I think you are so cool Terrible T."

"You cool too JaLisa I like the way you just chill."

"So when are you coming back to Miami?"

"Actually not for a few more months I'm scheduled for something here in the spring."

"Please let me know I'll definitely come out to support you."

"That's what I like to hear, thank you. That's why I asked you to come to New York to the show. Look everyone knows that Miz Thang' is my girl but I'm entitled to have friends."

"No problem in having friends Terrible T. it's just you're in the publics eye and everything you do is amplified one hundred times over."

"You telling me? You know JaLisa I enjoy just sitting here chillin wit you."

I looked over at his diamond encrusted watch and it's 3am. I'm not tired at all but I know damn well I have to be at work in five hours.

"What about breakfast you wanna go eat wit me when we leave here?"

"Yeah . . . Why not?"

The waiter brought us another bottle of Cristal and I had two more glasses we toasted to a new found friendship. We stayed about another hour before Terrible T. told Rashod that we were leaving to go have breakfast and that he will catch up wit him in New York. Jasmine and I hugged and she said she would call me later in the morning. Terrible T. said "I'll have my driver bring you back to your car on my way to the airport I'm supposed to be there at 6am."

"Cool"

We left out the back door and his driver was there waiting for us. We leave in a silver Bentley with black windows. I've never been in a Bentley before. I'm surprised when we pull into the Biltmore one of the oldest and most classy hotels in South Florida. We were the only ones in the restaurant at this time in the morning but that didn't stop us from ordering. Terrible T. ordered Belgium Waffles and a well done steak and I ordered fried potatoes and French toast. Shit we could have gone to IHOP for the prices they are charging us here. We have a table in a secluded area of the restaurant and the only light is from a single candle that's on the table. It was just like me to order something as simple as French toast from here the last time I came here with my job I ordered the jumbo shrimp and a small salad. I'm not really into trying new foods and they have a lot of shit that I never heard of on the menu.

~ RICHARD ~

I forgot to close the blinds last night so the sunrise woke me up. I thought I had been dreaming last night until I rolled over and Monica was silently sleeping next to me. There's a menu to the restaurant next to the bed in the top drawer so I pull it out and just randomly start to order from it. When I called the front desk they transfer me to the restaurant and I ordered pancakes, scrambled eggs, a fruit platter, biscuits with strawberry jam and coffee with cream on the side. I have no idea what Monica likes to eat so I'll let her choose. It took a half hour for the food to come and Monica didn't wake up till she heard the door. She is so beautiful with no make up or anything. I asked her "Are you hungry? I didn't know what you'd like."

There's a white guy that brings the food and when I try to pay him he said don't worry about it he'd charged it to the room. I gave him a tip anyway and thanked him. He kept looking at Monica and she gave him a look like "damn ain't you eva seen a woman wake up before!" She stretched and takes a few pieces of fruit and one pancake. She asks me "Are you okay with what happened last night?"

"Girl you put somethin on me."

"I just hope you're not havin regrets I know I came on pretty strong."

~ JaLisa ~

After breakfast the driver took me back to Club Bed to pick up the car. I promised Terrible T. that I would come to New York to see his show and we exchanged numbers. He leaned over and kissed me on my cheek and told me that I was beautiful before I got out the car. When I got into Richard's car it was 5:45am and no point in trying to go home and get some sleep because that was out of the question. I did go home to change and when I walked in I saw the answering machine light on. I picked up to check the message and it was Richard. He sounds worried, my cell phone is in my purse and it's off because my battery went dead. I have about an hour and half to get to work and since I can't ride the HOV I'm gonna need all that time just trying to get there. So I go through my closet to find something comfortable. Nothing tight and I must have on flat shoes. I jump in the shower and decided on a pant set I brought from a boutique a few weeks ago. I remember that I have class tonight after work so I had to run back in the house to grab my books. I don't know how I'm gonna make it though this day with no sleep.

I made it to work on time and that's a great relief. When I get to my desk I dial my time in and immediately start working on that report I left from last week. Brenda has walked passed my desk twice and I haven't looked up I know she's wondering how I'm gonna respond to her today but I don't have time for her shit. The third time that she walked passes she said, "JaLisa I know a quicker way that you complete that report I gave you last week."

"Oh really well you can pick the report off the printer because I'm already finish with that. All I need you to do is proof it for errors. I'll also emailed you a copy. Thanks." I said back with a dry ass smile.

She headed straight for the printer and went to her office and closed the door. I love to ruffle her feathers cause she thinks she knows every damn thing and she don't.

~ JASMINE ~

Last night JaLisa and I had the best time ever at the concert. Even though I was with Rashod at Club Bed I kept thinking about JaLisa and the way Terrible T. was looking at her. I was jealous because the way she was responding to him. I have never told her how I really felt about her but I have had the biggest crush on her forever and she doesn't even know it. I'm bisexual and I have never told my best friend about it. I don't know if I am even going to tell this girl how I feel about her.

Rashod and I went back to his place but I was so tipsy off the Cristal that I don't remember much that happened after we got there. I called out of work today because I knew damn well that I was not going to be up for taking no bodies shit today. I tried to call JaLisa once already but it went to her voice mail I need to know what happened after they left the club and is she really up for going to New York next weekend I would love to do some shopping up there.

~ RICHARD ~

Monica just left she had to go and set up for her seminars. I can't believe she wanted some more of me this morning but we ran out of condoms last night. She told me that she'd see me tonight at our opening show and she wished me luck. Before she left we kissed and she thanked me for making her feel so good last night. Shit I need to be thankin her ass. We have a sound check at noon so I'm just gon sit here and rub my balls and click this remote till it's time for the car to pick us up. I still haven't heard from JaLisa so I call her on her cell but it goes straight to voice mail so I dial her on her office phone to see if she made it into work.

"Thank you for calling TLC Incorporated."

"Hey baby I miss you I just wanted to know that you were okay."

"Yes baby I'm fine we just had a long night and my battery went dead on my cell."

"I know you can't talk long I just want to tell you how much I love you."

"I love you too baby can't wait till you come home."

"Okay at noon I have sound check and I know you have school tonight and you know a nigga first show tonight so I guess I won't talk to you till tomorrow."

"I love you baby good luck tonight."

"Thanks baby talk to you tomorrow."

~ JALISA ~

Lunchtime couldn't come soon enough I went and sat in the car, charged my cell phone up, leaned the seat back, turned the music on and dozed off to sleep. The sun feels so warm against my skin and I wish I could stay out here a little longer but I know I better not. I've been able to stay away from Brenda after I gave her that report and I want to keep it that way. If I want to go to New York next weekend I need to start planning now I could leave after my class on Saturday afternoon. After my phone finished charging it showed seven voice mail messages that I don't have time to listen to right now.

~ RICHARD ~

I know I won't be hollering at JaLisa tonight so when Monica invited herself ova afta the show I didn't think twice about hittin that ass one mo time but I told myself this was it. She came down to my room after we got back to the hotel from the afta party her and Resha' was drinkin like fish so she was all ova a nigga but I won't have that shit out in public with the press and shit. All a nigga needs is some pictures gettin back to JaLisa she would cut my d--- off. JT and Resha went to his room so Monica waited until they were inside then she came down here and knocked on my door. When I opened the door my eyes was bout to pop out my damn head. This chick actually walked through the hotel hall with a see through shirt on no bra or nuttin. She had on a matching pair of those boy shorts that they have in dem Victoria Secret catalogs that JaLisa always have laid around. I grabbed her arm and pulled her in the room.

"What the f--- you come out the room like that fo?"

She starts giggling and shit, "Cause I wanted to be comfortable!"

"What if somebody saw yo ass!"

"So, what if?"

"Look you know the press is gon be all up in a nigga shit jus lookin for somethin to tear me down and you walkin up in my shit lookin like this . . . that shit ain't cool!"

"Richard I leave this Friday my conferences are over then. I was jus havin a little fun. You should have seen your eyes. You looked so funny like I was your girl or something."

She then pointed to my d--- and said "He don't have a problem wit this outfit."

My d--- was hard as shit and damn she do look good as a mo f---a but she should know betta than that.

Monica pushes my back to the wall and lifted my T-Shirt ova my head. My pants was already loose cause I ain't have no belt on. She slides my pants and my boxers to my ankles. When she went for my d--- I lifted her off the floor.

"What are you doing Richard let me do this!"

"Nah I been out all day and ain't had no shower give me a minute."

I went and turned the shower on as hot as I could get it. All I keep thinkin bout is how hurt I would be if JaLisa did some shit like this to me. When I see her I'm gonna have some major makin up to do. Monica look fine as shit in that damn outfit but she should have been covered up before she came to my room JaLisa would neva do that shit. When I got out the shower Monica had a pack of condoms on the stand next to the bed. She was laying there with her hand inside her shorts rubbin her clit her hair laid out all ova the pillow. When she see me coming out da bathroom she started blushin and shit.

She asked, "You ready for me now?"

She tells me to come stand ova her while she's laying on her back. I ain't neva had no shit like this done to me she freaky as shit. She's suckin on a nigga like she gettin paid to do this shit. This time I couldn't hold back I bust all in her mouth and she drank erry drop of my nut.

"Got Damn!"

"You like that Richard?"

She don sucked a nigga dry but I'm still hard. She tears open the condom box wit her teeth and put it on for me. Now I'm on my back and she's ridin me like a stallion.

"This is some good ass p---- girl!"

Monica is cummin like crazy I can feel how wet she's gettin. She leaned down and started sucking on my neck.

"I'm gon miss you so much Richard! Ah! Shit!"

I grab her waist and pull her down on my d--- as hard as I can and she's still cumming like shit.

"Richard!"

"What? This is what you wanted ain't it?"

"Oh Richard! Yes!"

She screaming so loud I know you can hear her ass if you was comin down da hall. I flipped her ova afta she finished cumming and now I've got both her legs on the headboard this is my favorite position with her cause I keep staring in her face. When I lean down and kiss her on her lips I see a tear roll down the side of her face.

"What's wrong?"

"I may not ever see you again Richard."

Her talkin like this made me grind the shit out of her. I just start sayin some shit I know won't happen. But I don't want her to be cryin and shit.

"Look when I go on tour in ATL I'll come see you and you can come see me when you get down in Miami."

"I can Richard? You'll let me come see you but what about your girl?"

"I'll handle my girl."

Monica grabbed me around my neck and started slobbin a nigga down. She movin her ass all around and I swear this some good ass p----. I came again.

~ JALISA ~

I know Jasmine don called me a hundred times since she found out
Terrible T. handled all our reservations. He had his assistant book
our round trip flights and reserved our hotel room. Afta class today I
picked her up and we drove to the airport. We had first class seating and
all the luxury we could eva ask for. Jasmine called Rashod and he's already
there. He's staying in the same hotel that we are going to be in. I've never
stayed in an Embassy Suites before so I'm pumped. I didn't tell Richard I
was coming to town I wanted to surprise him. I requested three days off
from Brenda I told her it was a family emergency and she brought it. She
really did look concerned when I left outta there yesterday but whateva I
need this break.

As soon as we landed I called Terrible T. on his cell phone and he said
to take a cab to the hotel and he'll be there in an hour he's at the studio.
I am getting nervous but I really want to see him. Jasmine called Rashod
and he told her to come straight to his room and to bring her stuff with
her. When we pull into the hotel driveway my mouth drops open this
place is amazing. It's a block over from Times Square and is so elegant.
When we get out the cab the driver puts our bags on this push thing and
makes sure that we get inside. He takes us to the front desk to check in.
When I paid him and gave him his tip he disappeared. The lobby to the
hotel looks like a ball room with Crystal chandeliers and shit hanging
from the ceiling. I am so impressed. Jasmine called Rashod back and he's
in Suite 1151. She doesn't even walk with me to my room she just said call
me. This girl is so boosted I thought I had never been outta Miami before
but she is ready to pass out. The front desk attendant gave me my keycard

he said that everything had been taken care of. I am in the Penthouse Suite at the very top of the hotel.

So I walk into this oversized doorway and inside looks like a condo this place is huge with a kitchen, living room, bedroom and a king-sized bed! The first thing I did was run jump and roll around on the bed. I feel like a little kid. The phone ringing startles me.

"Hello."

"What's up JaLisa? It's T. I'll be there in a bit. I got held up at the studio. Are you hungry?"

"Yeah kinda, they tried to feed us on the plane but since it was my first time on one I was too nervous."

"So, are you nervous now?"

I looked at the phone and said, "No T. I ain't nervous."

"Good cause I don't bite unless you want me to."

"Nah, I'm cool. I can't wait to see you."

"Oh yeah?"

"Yeah T., I've been thinking about you ever since you dropped me off at my car that morning. This room is off the hook!"

"Good! I just wanna see you smile. It should be some stuff in the fridge. When I get there we can decide what we'll eat."

"Okay T. just don't keep me waiting too long."

"A'aight it's a bet."

I hung up the phone and I'm blushing from ear to ear. What does this man see in me, he has the baddest chick in the industry? I ran into the kitchen and almost broke something opening the fridge too fast. There are three bottles of Cristal, strawberries, whipped cream, chocolate-covered pecans, Vodka, grapefruit juice . . . How did he know I like this stuff? I grab the Vodka and grapefruit juice and pour myself a drink in one of the glasses on the counter. This is so cool. No one would believe this shit. I picked my purse up off the floor by the door and grabbed my cell to call Jasmine.

"Girl, I have died and gone to heaven!"

"Me too, JaLisa. This room is so tight and Rashod is spoiling me to death."

"Where is he now?"

"He's in the shower. We are going out soon."

"Come see my room while he's in the shower. You are not going to believe this shit."

"Okay, what's your room number?"

"Bitch I am in the Penthouse Suite!"

"What?"

"Hell yeah, come up here before Terrible T. gets here. I'll have the door open."

When Jasmine finally got up here she just spun around in the middle of the floor speechless. She walked around running her hands over the furniture like she was so impressed.

"My room is nice but it don't look shit like this."

"Bitch did you see the king-sized bed?"

"This shit is beautiful."

"Girl, come in here and look in the fridge. Let's have a drink before you go."

"Wow! Who put all this stuff in here?"

"How the hell do I know? Who told him that I like Vodka and grapefruit juice?"

"I remember you ordered one when we went to the show that night while we drank the Cristal."

"Damn Jasmine but he actually remembered."

"You are so lucky JaLisa you betta not mess this up trippin off Richard."

"Why you had to mention my baby? He would kill me if he knew what I was doing."

"That's exactly why you ain't gonna tell him. I hope you don't think his ass been faithful the whole time he been here."

"What? Why would you say that? I don't think he would do anything like that. It's all about the music to him."

"Okay let's just say he did. Please don't mess this up. JaLisa you deserve to be happy. Just enjoy yourself. You can go see Richard before we leave."

"I know I am. I was just looking through my bags to see what I should put on. I don't want to look like a freak when he walks in."

"Just put on something comfortable. Put on that tight black pant set. You know . . . the one that is soft when you touch it."

"Okay, I think I'll do that."

"I'm gonna take a shower. Girl, I have worked up a sweat jumping up and down in here. I am so excited."

"I know, me too. I'm out cause Rashod is waiting for me. I'll call you in the morning to see what we have planned. Rashod has some promotional stuff to do tomorrow. So we'll have some time to shop and go over to Times Square."

"Cool. Have fun tonight."

"Oh, believe me I will."

I gave her a bottle of Cristal for her and Rashod. I'm sure Terrible T. won't miss it. She let herself out and I walked into the bathroom. It looks like something from the "Lifestyles of the Rich and Famous." Everything in here is gold from the shower to the toilet and even the sink. I turned on the shower and it's so hot that beads of sweat popped up on my forehead. I love it hot but that is just damn scalding. When I got it to just like I like it I went to grab my little travel bag from my luggage. Now I can be nice and fresh when Terrible T. gets here. I am kinda nervous but that Vodka made me loosen up a little. While I shower I shave my pubic hair real low, especially around my clit ring. Shit, he ain't buy whipped cream and strawberries for nothing. I take a really quick shower because I don't want him to walk in on me. I put on my cutest panties set with the matching bra and slip into the soft outfit that Jasmine suggested. When Terrible T. finally walked in the door I was on the couch with my legs crossed Indian style sipping on my second glass of Vodka and grapefruit juice. We looked into each other's eyes as if we were long lost lovers. I hopped off the couch and jumped into his arms his coat and body was cold. The temperature has dropped since we arrived earlier. With his arms wrapped around my back we kissed and exchanged tongues like we've know each other forever. I am so moist right now and he goes from my lips to my ear to my neck as he whispers in my ear. "Did you miss me?"

"Yeah I thought of you every day just wondering what you were going to do with me."

"Shit I can think of a million and one things right now." He said as he licked his lips.

"I bet you can."

He walked around while he took off his coat and asked.

"So do you like this spot?"

"Yeah Terrible T. it's beautiful."

"I brought it a few months ago I know the owner of this place and he gave me a good deal. Whenever you want to come back you don't ever have to worry about a place to stay."

"You think you gonna want me to come back Terrible T.?"

"Shit I don't want you to have to leave."

He went and sat where I was sitting when he walked in and he held out his hand for me to come over. When I got close he grabbed my hand and sat me on his lap. His d--- is hard as shit and he's huge. I closed my eyes for a moment and took a deep breath. He's playing with my braids and biting on my neck. We started kissing again and I sat on him facing him and he said. "Damn JaLisa you are beautiful girl you know that?"

"Thanks Terrible T."

"You wanna go out or just stay in?"

"Whatever you want Terrible T. I came here for you."

He stood up with me still on him. My legs wrapped around his waist and he placed his hands on my ass he said, "I was trying to wait but I want you right now."

"I want you too Terrible T."

We started kissing as he carried me to the bedroom. He lays me on the bed and kisses my eyelids. From there he kisses my cheeks and bites on my ears. I am soaking wet right now and my panties are sticking to me. He slides my shirt over my head and holds my breasts. Terrible T. nibbles on both my breasts and licks down to my navel. I am getting so damn hot and I know he's not about to eat me out he just can't. He slides my panties and pants down and threw them on the floor. Well damn. He sees the clit ring and looks at me funny.

He said, "I didn't know you had one of these down here."

Terrible T. takes my ring in his mouth and sucks on my clit until my body goes weak. I should have known wit them juicy ass lips that he knows how to eat p----.

"Damn Terrible T. that feels so good."

He responds by making my legs shake. I really do not believe that I am here with Terrible T. and my legs are wrapped around his neck and he actually knows how to suck on me in all the right spots. It's totally different than when I'm with Richard. Richard sucks on me until I just can't take no more. But with Terrible T. I just want to keep cumming and cumming it's like continuous ecstasy.

"Terrible T. I'm cumming!"

"Keep cumming that's what you supposed to be doing."

"You're making me feel so good Terrible T."

"I just wanna see you smile."

I know he has been sucking on me for like thirty minutes and I am cumming all over the place. My mind wonders around the Penthouse and how beautiful it is. My body is so relaxed and my mind wonders to a tropical island somewhere it's amazing how I just close my eyes and fantasize. I deserve this life with Terrible T. but I know he can't be serious about me. After the foreplay he lifted me to the top of the bed and asked me if I wanted to make love to him. He said, "It's totally your choice. I respect you and if you wanna stop here I'm cool with that."

Before he could say anything else I got on top of him and kiss him like he's my man. I unhook the belt in his pants and slide it out with one swoop. I then take the belt and tie his hands together and tie them tight to the headboard. He is all smiles. He lifts up as I unbutton his pants and push them on the floor with his shoes. He's wearing white boxers with black eight balls on them and I slide them off and put them under the pillow and tell him.

"Those are mine."

He just laughs as I go down on him and wrap my entire mouth around his big ass d---. I would have never guessed that he would be this big. When I roll my tongue around the head he moves a little.

"You like that?"

He doesn't say word but he closes his eyes and nods. I can taste him and he's so sweet.

He says "Oh yeah . . . just like that don't move."

I proceed with caution because I don't know if he's gonna cum or not. He is so huge that I'm almost choked.

"Terrible T. I wanna make you cum."

"Shit you keep doin what you doin and you gon see it."

I jump up and run to the kitchen and grab a bottle of Cristal, the strawberries and the whipped cream. Before I go back to the room I open the bottle and grab a glass from the counter. When I get back the room Terrible T. is just laid back in his same position with his eyes closed. I pour him a half glass of Cristal and hold it to his mouth so he can drink. He drinks it all in one swallow and licks his lips afterward. I spray whipped cream in the bowl with the strawberries and scoop some up and feed one to him he bites it and licks his lips again. I take another one with whip cream and rub it on him and he moves a little because it's really cold. I bite it and suck on him with the strawberry in my mouth and he starts to moan.

"Yeah baby just like that. Don't move."

The next thing I know he releases all in my mouth and opens his eyes. He's surprised that I drank every drop of him. I untie his hands and he grabs me and we kiss. His kisses make me weak it's like he's really into me. He reaches on the floor for his pants and pulls some condoms out of his wallet he says, "Just in case you wanted to give me some."

"I would love to."

I lay with the sheets pulled up to my neck until he finished puttin on the condom and we kissed again. He whispered in my ear, "You sure you want this."

"I'm a big girl Terrible T."

"I like that."

He slides inside me and my eyes close he pulls me close to him by my waist and he is making love to me and I can not believe it. He is passionately making love to me.

"Oh Terrible T.!"

"Yes JaLisa?"

"I'm afraid of being hurt."

"I won't hurt you JaLisa I just want to add to your life not bring you any more drama."

"Terrible T. you feel so good inside me."

"I feel exactly what you feel ever since the first time I saw you at my show. I was like yo I've gotta have her."

"But . . ."

"You don't worry about anything, whenever you want to see me or be with me I'm here with just one call."

"Oh Terrible T. you don't mean that."

"Damn JaLisa you feel so good."

"I'm scared Terrible T."

"Don't be scared baby. I won't hurt you. I won't let you get hurt."

He rolls over and lets me ride him he looks into my eyes and says, "Whateva you want you got it."

"Terrible T. you're just saying that."

"I get what I like and I like you JaLisa."

"Please don't hurt me Terrible T."

"You got my word."

As he says that he pulls me down on top of him and allows me to feel every inch. He grabs my face and we start kissing again. I'm riding him like it's my duty and I believe him I'm sure he can have any woman he wants.

"Oh Terrible T. I'm cumming."

"Me too."

We lay for a while without moving just holding each other and I honestly believe that I am fulfilling whatever it is that he is missing in his life right now and I know he's doing the same for me. I don't know whose stomach growled first but we both are hungry he asks, "You wanna order room service or you wanna go out."

"It's too cold I ain't used to this weather we can stay in?"

~ RICHARD ~

M y cell rings and the number that shows up is from Something Else's office here in New York.

"Hello."

"Hey Richard, what's happening this is Todd."

Todd is one of the producers that helped me get signed and made sure that a nigga got a proper deal. Any time he calls this Yankee talking money.

"What's up Todd what can I do for you?"

"That's a great attitude to have my man I can get you some extra cash if you can agree to do me a huge favor tomorrow."

"Tomorrow cool I ain't got shit to do till Tuesday when we do our next show in Manhattan."

"Okay this is the deal I can get you $10,000 cash in your hands if you can open up for a major entertainer tomorrow. They have already decided that they were going to be late but they don't want the audience waiting that long. All I need you to do is to get on the stage and do your thing for about thirty minutes maybe not even that long. So what do you think?"

"Yo for 10 g's you got it just tell me when and where and are the other artist coming wit me?"

"It's going to be in Times Square and I need you to be there at 6pm you will go on at about 7 but the stage manager says he needs you earlier. And to answer your last question this gig is just for you my man this is your spot light."

"Cool I'm game!"

"The driver will be at your hotel at 5 o'clock."

That's tight not only am I gonna get my check from these shows I been doing a nigga gon get some extra's I like that shit. I've just been in my room chillin since Monica left yesterday. She came in here all tore up before she left said she needed to be like that for the flight home. She was asking me was I gonna keep in touch wit her and shit and I said yeah. I gave her my cell number and she gave me the number to her Mama's house cause she still lives at home. See that's the shit I mean none of these chicks compare to my JaLisa she's holdin it down. I'm glad she's gone I'm beginning to lose it. I ain't been talking to JaLisa like I want to and now erry time I call her that damn voice mail shit picks up. Damn I forgot to ask Todd who I was opening up for. Ah f--- it I don't give a shit if I was opening for Michael Jackson right about now 10 g's guaranteed.

I hopped up and threw on a pair of jeans and a T-shirt so that I can run down to the bar and a couple of Heinekens.

JT's at the bar and dis nigga look bent like he don lost his best friend or some shit.

"Yo what's up?"

"Ain't shit just bored."

"Yo ass ain't bored you miss that chick Resha's"

"Nah yo."

"Who do you think you foolin?"

"Man shorty all up in a nigga's head and shit."

"Yeah I feel you on that."

"She don called me bout ten times since they don went back home."

"So you gon keep in touch?"

"That's what I been thinkin bout you know I got a girl at home but she trippin like shit bout me being here. I told her it's all about the cash but she ain't buying it."

"Damn yo you can't much blame her she knows how scandalous these chicks are."

"That ain't even it she wants to be here but I can't have that if she was here I could not focus on shit but her naggin ass."

"Yo I only wish my girl wanted to be here with me I'd have her as on the first flight. She just got so much shit goin on that she can't jus up and leave all that."

"We only got one more week here and then we go back home but right now I don't even want to go back home. Have you heard if we gon have any more shows coming up once we go home."

"Nah I ain't heard shit. I got this solo shit to do tomorrow. I'm thinkin they gon let us do our own thing once we go back home. This shit was just to see who was gonna hold up. Have you seen Lil Mike and Raymond?"

"I ain't seen dem nigga's since our last show."

I gave JT some dap and left him drinkin in his sorrows at the bar. I need to go ova to the studio and listen to some tracks that I think I wanna do tomorrow. I went up to my room and grabbed my sweat hoody and my coat cause it's cold as a mo f---a outside. When I got to the front lobby it's a cab already out there so I hop in it and ask him to run me down about ten blocks. The studio is not too far from here but it's too cold to walk.

~ JALISA ~

fter dinner came Terrible T. said, "Let's get in the Jacuzzi."

"Oh that sounds good."

I pinned my braids up and fill the Jacuzzi with one of the little bubble bath bottles that's in the bathroom.

I yelled into the living room, "Terrible T. it's ready."

He came in carrying the rest of the bottle of Cristal along with the bowl of strawberries and whipped cream.

I looked at him with a smile and said, "You want some more of me?"

"All day and all night."

I filled the Jacuzzi up so high that when we both got in water spilled over to the floor. Terrible T. said, "Don't worry about that the maid will clean it in the morning."

This shit is the life I came over to his side and started feeding him strawberries and he did the same to me. He poured me a drink and we just sat and talked.

"So where do we go from here?" Terrible T. asked.

"Well I love Richard but he keeps telling me not yet. I would love to be a part of your life Terrible T. but I know it's very risky with the press and all. I don't know where we go from here I just want to bask in this moment forever but I know it's not possible."

"Yeah this moment would be nice but we'd get all wrinkled and white sittin in all this water. And I don't want to be either wrinkled or white."

"So when I go back home will you ever get a chance to come down and see me."

"Yeah I know for a fact that I will be there in the spring but at the first of the year I have to go on tour across seas so I know it won't be before then."

"Damn Terrible T. you live such an exciting life all I do is go to work and school."

"Don't feel bad you stick with me and you will travel more you have to stick with that school thing though that's where it's at for us black people . . . either that or music or sports."

"And I ain't good at either one of those so I betta stick with school."

I sat my glass down and leaned my head back and closed my eyes and rocked my head back and forth to a rhythm I had in my head.

Terrible T. said, "What you thinkin bout over there."

"Just you and this . . . I've never experienced nothing like this I just wish I could live like this every day."

"Believe me you just keep doing what you doing and you will have all this and then some."

He pulled me on top of him and I just sat on his lap. We kissed and my body started throbbing for him. Damn I want some more but we are in all this water with no condoms. The water is so warm and it's making me horny as hell. He kissed my eyelids and said, "Let me make it all better for you."

"How you gonna do that Terrible T.?"

"Whateva you need I'm just a call away I know a lot of people in a lot of places and can get anything I want."

He got out of the Jacuzzi drippin wet and wrapped up with a towel. He held out a towel and wrapped me up in it then swooped me off my feet and carried me into the room. He laid me down and opened my legs and started sucking all of my stress away. This man has a gift and it's not only making money but what he's doing is a talent. This shit feels so good I want to start crying.

"Oh Terrible T. you have a talent baby."

He stopped sucking on me and burst out laughing. He said, "JaLisa you crazy and I like it."

I lay back and allow my mind to drift off like I did earlier and all I can picture is Richard. I miss him so much and I will never be able to be with Terrible T. the way I can be with Richard and it makes me sad because it's like nothing even matters right now Terrible T. is making me feel so good. I shake Richard out of my head only for him to pop back up in it. Terrible

T. is sucking on my clit and sliding his fingers in and out of me and this shit is the bomb. When I let out one of the biggest orgasms I have ever had he just laid his head on my stomach with his eyes closed, I'm sure he has his own demons to fight with. He has to have a conscience and knows that what he's doing is not right.

"Terrible T. let's get under the covers I'm cold baby."

We got under he covers and he held me from behind in the nude. I was everything he needed tonight and he was the same. We both doze off and what is so wrong feels so right.

I wake up and its 2 o'clock in the morning and Terrible T. is still here holding me. I was sure that he would have left by now but he hasn't. He invited me to a show that he has to do tomorrow that's not too far from where we are staying. I'm going to ride there with Jasmine and Rashod just because I can't come in there with him.

~ RICHARD ~

T he driver picked me up on time and we pulled up in the back of this two-story club that I am going to be performing at. It has to be at least five hundred people here already. The bass from the music vibrated through me when we went into the emergency entrance. This dude in a suit said, "You must be Richard?" and he took me to another suit that had everything laid out on his desk. The money was there in rubber bands. I take it he's Italian cause they the only folks that have set ups like this one.

The Italian dude says, "Hey Richie what's up man I'm John. Are you ready to warm the club up for Terrible T.?"

"Yo, my name is Richard!"

"Okay Richard . . . Mr. Terrible T. will be here in one hour his assistant called and said that Terrible T. wants the club to be hype by the time he gets here. I hope you're good."

He took the rubber banned money and slides it across the table.

"It's all there trust me so are you ready? You have about fifteen minutes before you go on. We have a dressing room downstairs if you need to get yourself together."

I took the money and put it in my pockets and my pants started to fall off my ass. He gave me a lock with a key attached and said, "There's a locker in the dressing room if you need to store anything in it."

The bass from the club has my head rockin not to mention I'm walkin around with 10 g's and a little as lock. I had no idea that I would be opening for Terrible T. this shit is huge. JaLisa would not believe this shit. Damn I wish she was here. When I got to the dressing room there's bottles of Cristal everywhere I turned.

"Who ordered this?"

There's a knock at the door before it opens.

"Hi Richie I'm Veronica, John's sister he said I could find you here. I'm gonna be introducing you in ten minutes so I need you to be ready. You can help yourself to anything in here. The Cristal is compliments from Terrible T. he wanted to tell you thank you for coming in on such short notice. He also wants you to stick around after the show if you'd like so that he can meet you."

She wouldn't stop talking so I didn't even bother to correct her with the Richie shit. Veronica opened a bottle of Cristal and poured a glass for me and her and held it up for a toast.

"Here's to better days Richie."

"To betta days Veronica."

I took all the money out of my pockets and put it in the locker, locked it and stuck the key in the little pocket in my jeans. I went over to the little sink and splashed water on my face.

"You ready Richie?"

"Yo, stand outside the door and give me like five minutes."

"Okay Richie I'll be right outside the door."

As soon as the door closed I closed my eyes and said a prayer, "Lord you know this is big and can make or break my career. I need you to give me strength to make it thru this one and yo boy will owe you one big. Amen."

I followed Veronica up to the backstage and she introduced me.

"Coming to the stage all the way form Miami, Florida is Richard Douglas which I like to call Richie cause his pockets are phat."

The ladies in the crowd went wild afta she said that. She walked to me as I walked out on da stage. I gave my all. The DJ already had my music so I just had to lay down the verses. When I got to my third song I swear on my life that I was seeing shit. It looked like JaLisa and Jasmine was sitting at the bar but I know that ain't right. When I looked again they was gone. I just kept on flowing until Veronica gave me a signal that I could wrap it up. Before I left the stage I gave the info where they could get a nigga's new CD and the website to check me out on line. When I finally got backstage Veronica was there waiting she said that John wanted me to come back to his office.

"Richie you were so great I didn't know you could flow like that."

When I walked up the stairs I could hear her introducing Terrible T. and the crowd went crazy. I didn't get that but it's all good. I will one day. I walked into John's office again ad he said, "Man Richie you were awesome how would you like to perform here every Friday for the month of January?"

"Yo, are you serious?"

"Yes, man the club loves you I'll pay you real nice Richie."

"I think I can do that I jus have to check with my producer before I put it on paper I don't know what day got comin up."

"Okay Richie but before you leave give me your number I can call you directly if you are free to come here I would rather work directly with you instead of the Record Company."

"Cool!"

"Richie are you going to stick around and wait for Terrible T. he wanted to talk to you. He said that if you couldn't that he would understand and he could call you."

"Nah I'll hang out here for a lil bit."

I went back down stairs to the dressing room and drank damn near the rest of the bottle that we opened before I went on stage. I unlocked the locker and grabbed all my loot and jus chilled. There's a speaker outside the room and I can hear Terrible T. still performing. He's tearin it up.

~ JaLisa ~

I grabbed Jasmine from the bar and ran to the bathroom as soon as I heard Richard on stage.

"Girl what is he doing here Terrible T. is here tonight?"

"I don't know JaLisa. Girl calm down you gon pass the f--- out if you don't chill."

"Chill! Chill! How in the hell can I chill and I been sexin Terrible T. all night? Then I come up in here and Richard is on the Got Damn stage this shit can't be real. Bitch pinch me cause I am seeing shit!"

"You ain't seeing shit that was him."

We left the bathroom and stood in line to get into VIP. The dude at the door was turning people away and we got to the front of the line and he let us in. I sunk down on the oversized couch and put my head in my hands.

"I feel like such an ass Jasmine."

"Girl how you gon say that you didn't know Richard was gonna be here."

"I know I didn't but I don't belong here I should have never agreed to come I'm supposed to be in Miami right now."

With tears rolling down my face I said to Jasmine, "You can stay but I'm going back to the hotel."

"Girl at least wait till after Terrible T. performs."

"Hell f--- no I'm outta here!"

When I stood up my head started pounding so I sat back down. I can't even think. Richard left the stage and not too long afta that Terrible T. came out.

"Jasmine we've gotta get outta here please let's go."

We caught a cab back to the hotel and Jasmine came to my room.

"Girl what if he saw me?"

"JaLisa stop trippin that nigga did not see you it was so many people in that club believe me he did not see you. We jumped up so fast and ran into the bathroom anyway so don't worry."

"Terrible T.'s gonna ask me why I didn't stick around."

"JaLisa just tell him the truth he'll understand."

"The truth, what do you mean?"

"I mean tell him you didn't know Richard was gonna be there and that he's the boyfriend you've been telling him about."

"Like that?" I asked.

"Just like that girl."

"I wanna call him so bad to tell him that I miss him and I'm here and that I want to see him."

"That would be a mistake because he's gonna want to know what are you doing here and what if he did see us it just doesn't look right."

"Now you're sayin what if he saw us."

My stomach got so weak. I ran to the bathroom but didn't make it to the toilet. I threw up all over the bathroom floor, I felt so dizzy.

"JaLisa you okay!" Jasmine called from the living room.

"Girl get up let me run you a bath."

I'm on my knees in front of the toilet when she pulls me up. Jasmine gave me a hug and told me to stop crying. She put the top down on the toilet and sat me down while she ran me a bath. I felt so bad and my stomach hurts like shit. After she finished running the bath she helped me undress and put me in the tub. Jasmine left out the bathroom and came back with a lit candle that she found out in the living room. She sat it on the side of the tub and turned out the bathroom light.

She said, "You just stay here and relax cause you stressed out and you stressin me out."

I heard her on the phone but I don't know who she's talkin to, maybe Rashod.

I had dozed off in the tub and Jasmine came in and turned on the light. She'd been down stairs to the gift shop and got me some saltine crackers and a ginger ale. I didn't even know she left out. She said that Terrible T. called and was asking why we didn't stick around to the end of the show. Jasmine told him I wasn't feeling well and it was something I ate. Terrible T. told her that he would be over but it was gonna be late.

He asked her did I need anything and she told him I would be fine. When Jasmine was telling me about Terrible T. all I could think about was seeing Richard on that stage and I know he had to see us. I know he spoke to Terrible T. I hope I didn't come up in the conversation. Jasmine lay in the bed beside me and we watched S.W.A.T. she rubbed my stomach after I ate the crackers and ginger ale. My head is spinning so I closed my eyes and drifted off to sleep.

It's after 1am when Terrible T. comes in the door. I heard him come through the door but I lay as still as I could like I was paralyzed. I heard him take off his coat and put his keys on the table in the front room. As he got closer to the room I heard him trip over something and he said, "Shit!"

When he made it to the room it was still and dark. Terrible T. sat beside me on the bed he said, "JaLisa, you sleep?"

I ignored him. He rubbed his fingers in my braids and said again, "JaLisa you sleep?"

I rolled over and opened my eyes without saying a word. He took the remote and turned the TV on. He pushed the mute button and said, "Baby you okay Jasmine told me you got sick."

"Yeah . . . I'm okay now I . . . I was feeling real bad earlier."

He rubbed his hand across my forehead and then laid his hand on my stomach as warm tears ran down my face.

"What's wrong baby did I do something? Do you want to go to the hospital?"

"No we just need to talk."

"I'm here we can talk now. What's up?"

"Well you know that guy that I've been telling you that I'm dating? He was at the club tonight."

"Oh yeah, you saw him there?"

"Yes, his name is Richard."

"You mean the one everybody keeps calling Richie. The one that performed before I did? Are you serious?"

"Very serious."

I couldn't stop the tears from running down my face.

"That cat is cool."

"Yeah he's real cool and I am so wrong."

"It's okay baby. Damn I see why you rolled out."

"Terrible T. I don't know what to do."

"It's all good baby but whether you wit that cat or not I like you. You are so cool JaLisa and I want to remain in touch with you. I talked to Richard afta my show and he agreed to do a couple of openings for me next month. I told him I could keep him busy because I have a lot of work here in New York."

"So that means he's gonna be in New York more?"

"Yeah, that's what it sounds like." Terrible T. said.

I closed my eyes and Terrible T. kissed me on my lips and he asked, "Can I make you feel better?"

I put my arms around his neck and kissed him like he was my man. I told him "I'm going back home tomorrow morning. I have to get back to Miami."

"Just stay another day I'll clear my schedule and we can spend the day together do this for me before you leave."

"Okay Terrible T. but just one more day I have to go back home."

As we kissed he sucked on my bottom lip and said, "I know he's your man but I wanna be your other nigga."

"Terrible T. you're crazy."

"No, I'm serious."

We kissed and started sucking on my neck. He licked between my breasts and stared kissing on my stomach. He moved to my toes and my entire body caught chills. Terrible T. sucked on my thighs while I bit my bottom lip. He said, "Can I taste you?"

"Yes Terrible T."

I don't believe he's sucking on me like it's really gonna be our last time together. I keep thinking about Richard. Terrible T. has my legs shakin already. I love the way he's makin me feel right now. My body is so relaxed.

~ RICHARD ~

I've been calling JaLisa at home and on her cell and she's not answering I hope errythang is alright. I waited for Terrible T. last night and he came down to my dressing room. He asked if I wanted to open some shows for him. And I was like "Hell Yeah!" I tried not to seem too hype but I am. We supposed to be hooking up and doin some stuff in the studio and I'm all for that. When I got back to the hotel last night that nigga JT was at the bar talking bout he's gon drop the tour and go back home. I ain't dropping shit I'm trying to get this paper and that's all I'm worried about.

Monica's been callin like crazy I had five messages from her last night talking bout she miss a nigga and she can't wait till the next time I hit that ass. My cell rings so I look at the number I thought it was Monica again but its Something Else.

"Yo."

"Hey Richard this is Todd."

"What's up man?"

"You, that's what's up!"

"What you mean?"

"Man John from that club you did last night has been calling me all morning. Not to mention Terrible T.'s assistant. Are you ready to blow up?"

"I was born ready!"

I could hear Todd smiling through the phone this cracker is bout that cash and I know he gon make sure I gets mine.

"Okay here it is. I've been talking to the Executive Producer here and he wants you to do a video. That way we can air it on BET, MTV and VH1 your audience will be broader with a video once the video hits the

72

radio will play you more. So do you have any video idea's, and have you thought about which song you want for the video?"

"Man Todd this shit is happening so fast I don't have a clue what to do first."

"Okay I know it's early still so do this I will have a driver come pick you up at noon and we can brainstorm and come up with some ideas here at the office. You think of the direction that you will feel comfortable going in and we will make it happen."

"That's a bet."

"Hey Richard, Terrible T. has agreed to be featured in your first video so we must make it HOT!"

"You got it Todd I'll be there at noon."

This some crazy shit but they say this is how it happens one day you ain't shit and ain't got shit and the next day you on and you the man. The video gon have to be done here in New York cause I know they gon want it to be fast. My phone rings again and this them it's JaLisa.

"Hey baby where you been? You alright I been trying to call you the last two days. What's up?"

"Hi baby I miss you. I've been running from class to work and over to my Mama's house helping her out."

"Oh okay but why you ain't answering your cell?"

"Cause baby it hasn't been working right it keeps forwarding to my voice mail."

"It's all good baby as long as I'm talking to you now. Baby I have some great news."

"Oh yeah?"

"Hell yes baby a nigga blowin up in New York."

"Damn baby I'm so happy for you."

"For me? No baby this here is fo us."

"I did this show for Terrible T. last night and I was seeing shit cause I swear I saw you and Jasmine."

"You miss me that's all baby."

"You right about that but listen to this after Terrible T. went on we talked about me doing some more openings for him and he talking about being on my album."

"Damn baby that's right."

"We bout to be big JaLisa and this is all for you baby."

"Thank you Richard. Richard I love you."

"Not yet JaLisa but believe me baby you will."

"Alright baby I gotta go I'm at work so jus call me on my cell later. I have class tonight and then I'm going back ova Mama's house."

"Okay, we'll talk tonight."

Damn I miss my baby. She's workin so hard and doin the school thang I just wanna make thangs betta fo her.

~ JaLisa ~

I hated having to lie to Richard but I couldn't tell him that I'm here in New York he would flip. I called him while Terrible T. was in the shower. When I heard the water turn off. I told Richard that I had to go. I'm already dressed Terrible T.'s takin me out today. When he got dressed we rode the elevator down to the basement garage where his black tinted Mercedes was waiting for us. We drove out of the city and went on the Highway. We must have driven about forty-five minutes to this huge Mansion.

"Where are we Terrible T.?"

"This is one of my houses."

"Damn Terrible T. this is beautiful."

"So are you."

"What we doing here?"

"I had a few people come over so that you can get pampered."

"What?"

"Yeah you need to relax you have been so tense."

When we pull into the circle driveway this tall Spanish chick with long black hair opens the door.

Terrible T. says, "That's Rosie she will be your servant for the day."

"My what?"

"Just let her do whatever she wants to do to you believe me she will hook you up."

"Terrible T.?"

"JaLisa you deserve this baby, you are too up tight and I need you to relax a little."

As we walked inside my mouth dropped. This place is amazing there's Persian rugs on the floors and artwork on the walls. He has a Cathedral ceiling with chandeliers and everything. Terrible T. left me with Rosie and kissed me on the lips and went up the spiral stair case.

Rosie said, "Hi MaMa I'm Rosie."

"Hi Rosie I'm JaLisa."

Rosie took me down this long hallway off to the left side of the house and brought me to this room that looked like it could be a library. There were books on shelves on each wall there's a cherry wood desk and a computer in here too. Rosie went over to the computer and typed in a few keys and told me to undress and put on this white terrycloth robe. I did as I was instructed. When she finished with the computer it played this Spanish music. Rosie saw my expression and said, "Its okay MaMa after this song something more relaxing will play."

She told me to lie down on the long white table that was over by the window. I sat on the table with my robe all tight and Rosie said, "Loosen up MaMa lay down on your stomach and open the robe."

I closed my eyes and did as she asked. She was right the next song that played was slow and more like Jazz, Rosie took my arms out the robe and pulled it down to my ass. She poured this liquid on my back and as soon as it touched my skin I felt a warm sensation. Rosie's fingers feel like little magic wands. My body went from tense to relax before the song finished playing. She started at my shoulders and went down to my arms she took each hand and messaged the inside of my palm and turned it over and messaged my knuckles. She went back to my shoulders and worked her way down to the small of my back. Rosie lifted the robe and lay it across my ass as she messaged my thighs down to my feet. I started to doze off as she did her thang. She started at my neck this time and did the entire routine again. When she finished I said, "Thank you Rosie I needed that."

She said, "No problem MaMa any friend of Terrible T.'s is a friend of mine."

We walked out of that room into another and this one was more like a playroom. There's a huge flat screen on the wall and a pool table in the middle of the floor. Video games sat to the side but they were unplugged. Rosie had a little table set up with a chair on each side. She told me to have a seat while she set up. When she came back into the room Rosie was carrying a foot message spa filled with bubbles and told me to stick my feet in it. The water was nice and hot and very relaxing. She left again and came back with two white manicure trays and told me to soak my hands in them I did as I was told. She messaged my hands and feet and gave me a French manicure on my hands and toes. I love it and I didn't even have to tell her what I wanted. When Rosie finished with me she helped me get dressed. She sat my shoes at the front door so I wouldn't mess up my toes and said, "Let's tour the house and find Terrible T."

I walked from room to room in amazement. I've never been in anything like this before. I love watching Cribs on TV but to actually be standing here seeing it for my own eyes was something very different. We found Terrible T in his studio at the very top of the house he said he was listening to some new tracks.

He asked, "So you relaxed now?"

"Yes Terrible T. I'm very relaxed thanks to Rosie."

Rosie smiled and left us alone she disappeared somewhere in the house.

Terrible T. asked, "Okay you ready I have someone that waiting for us?"

"Where ever you want to take me Terrible T. I'm following your lead."

We got downstairs and Rosie was there waiting for us my toenails were dry now so she helped me put my shoes on.

She held my face and kissed me on both cheeks and said, "You're a beautiful girl JaLisa I hope you enjoyed."

"I did, thanks again Rosie."

She watched as Terrible T. and I walked out to the car and once we pulled off she closed the door.

"Thank you so much Terrible T. I need that."

"I know baby it only gets better."

~ RICHARD ~

I couldn't get to the studio fast enough when the driver came to get me. We have another show to do tomorrow night so I was writing some new shit for that and thankin bout what I want to do for this video. When we finally get here I hopped out the truck and didn't even look back to see if the door had shut. I went straight to Todd's office and we walked to the conference room where the Executive Producer was along with two other white chicks that I never seen before. Errybody introduced them selves and Todd sat licking his lips and rubbing his hands together. I knew something was up but I was not expecting what came next. Todd said, "We have some good news and some bad news which one would like to hear first Richard?"

"Ah . . . first give me the bad."

"Okay the bad news is that we no longer own your contract here at Something Else. Your contract has been sold to Def Jam records to the President Terrible T. himself."

"What? I'm confused can you do that?"

"Well in your contract section 21 article 15 states that if Something Else finds a more lucrative deal for our artist we don't even have to discuss the change we can just do it."

"Okay so what do that mean for me Todd?"

"That means that your contract has been sold for 1.5 million dollars and you as the artist are entitled to 1.3 million of those dollars. This is far more than we can ever pay you Richard. This is a very good deal."

"So you mean I am a millionaire just like that?"

"Just like that Richard all you have to do is sign on the dotted line."

"Before I sign anythang what do I have to do to get this million?"

"Richard read my lips we have already done this for you. You are a millionaire and the money is being transferred into your account as we speak."

"But I thought I was coming here to work on video ideas."

"You are here to do that also we have to do your first video since the songs that you made for us are on your previous contract but after that you are no longer obligated to do anything else for us. As far as the rest of the tour it is totally up to you. The tour would be just extra money for you."

"I'm confused?"

"An hour ago we received a call from Terrible T. himself requesting to have the rights to your new album and he wants to work with you personally on it."

"Did he say why?"

"He says that he's been listening to your tracks and you are a gold mine."

"Damn, I don't know what to say."

"Just please tell us you are happy."

"Happy I'm about to lose my f----- mind."

"Just sign Richard."

I took the pen and sign all of my rights away to Terrible T. for 1.3 million dollars and I am speechless. Why would he do this for me? I know my shit is good but damn is it really like that? JaLisa is not gonna believe this shit at all I am not gonna be able to tell her this shit on the phone I'mma have go home and sit her down and tell her some shit like this. Errybody at the table stood up and clapped after I signed off on the contract. My head is spinning like shit and my palms all sweatin and shit.

Todd says, "So now to the video. Have you come up with anything?"

"Yeah I want to be in the studio with the mike just spittin lyrics. From the studio we can show shots of Times Square and other shots of New York City. I want the entire video to be shot here in New York."

"That's a great idea Richard and it will save you a whole lot of money."

That's all this cracker thinks about is money. But it's all good shit I'm all for savin. We walked down to the elevator and took it to the next floor where the studio is and Todd told me to feel it out and he would have the cameras up soon. I went inside the booth and told the dude behind the equipment to play the track to my single so I could practice. Todd sent the camera crew and they said all I had to do was act like I was singing cause they don't record sounds they just record me. The track played and I laid it down on the first try, no retakes, no rewinds just like that and I was out. The rest is up to the tricks of the camera and the shots they get in Times Square. When I got finished Todd told me to go back to the hotel and get my thoughts together he said that he would send over the video tape once they finished with it and to let him know by tonight if I was doing the show tomorrow.

~ JaLisa ~

Terrible T. wasn't lying when he said he had a surprise for me. He took me back to the city and we pulled in the back of this boutique. When we got in three white women all size three swarmed me. One took my measurements 34-24-34 something like that and she went off to find clothes. The next one sized my feet and brought back two pairs of Monolos one of which I saw in the magazine last month. The third woman fitted me with diamond earrings and a diamond tennis bracelet. She came back with a gold necklace with a heart shaped diamond heart on it. I feel like Cinderella. I looked over at Terrible T. and he's punching in something on his Palm Pilot. The outfits and shoes went in bags and the jewelry stayed on. I had no idea to expect all this from Terrible T. I can't wait to tell Jasmine she ain't gon believe this shit. How am I gonna explain all this shit to Richard? Terrible T. comes up behind me and wraps his arms around my waist and kissed me on my neck. He said, "You happy now JaLisa?"

"Yes Terrible T. every moment that I'm wit you I'm happy."

"But you still have to go home don't you?"

"Yes Terrible T. I need to leave tomorrow."

He turned me around and said, "So what can I do to make you stay a little longer?"

"Just let me go and I promise I'll be back."

I didn't see him pay or anything but he must have because we left the boutique with all my stuff. I feel so spoiled right now.

Terrible T. asked, "You hungry?"

"Yes but I want to go back to the hotel."

Terrible T. looked in my eyes and smiled and said, "I like the sound of that."

It takes us fifteen minutes to get back to the hotel from the boutique. When we got back Terrible T. ordered us food and I called Jasmine on my cell phone.

She answered, "What's up girl you feel betta?"

"Yeah much better me and Terrible T. been out all day."

"I know cause I been trying to call."

"We have to leave tomorrow girl I have to get back to reality."

"I wonder why you want to go back so soon?"

"Girl this ain't my life this somebody else's shit I gotta go back home."

"Rashod said he ready to go back too he said it's too cold here."

"When we get off the phone call the airport and see what the earliest flight back is."

"Okay but you a busta."

"What? Why you say that?"

"Cause you ready to run home so soon."

"Girl I got work, school and a life I have to get back to."

"Okay, okay I'll do it. I'll call you back."

When I got off the phone I went and sat by Terrible T. he's watching the news.

"Terrible T. Jasmine's gonna call the airport to find the earliest flight back."

He pulled me on his lap and started licking inside my ears and down to my neck.

He said, "I'm gonna miss you."

"Terrible T. I'll be back or you can come see me."

"I will."

I could feel his d--- getting hard and it was turning me on like shit. I went and got undressed and got a pair of my shoes out the bag and put them on. I took the remote and turned the TV off and turned on the music. As the music played I felt it in every inch of my body and started dancing for him naked. He's loving every minute of this. My body moved to every beat in the song. He got up off the sofa and started dancing with me. I undressed him and watched him put on a condom from his wallet. He sat down on the sofa and I got on top of him and slid my body down and rode him he's making more noises than me. Terrible T. put both of his hands on my waist and pulled me down on him. This shit feels so good.

Terrible T. says, "I'm gonna miss you so much. I'm gonna miss this so much."

"Me too Terrible T. Me too."

Terrible T. picked me up and laid me down on the sofa on my back and did one of the things that he does best.

"Damn Terrible T. I'm gonna miss this."

"So won't you stay?"

"Terrible T. if I could I would but I have to go back home I have to check on my Mama."

"Okay I understand."

He stopped sucking on my clit and started grinding the shit out of me like this was gonna be it. This was really gonna be the last time. I'm so wet you can hear him going in and out of me. Terrible T. stops cause there's a knock on the door. Its room service and we totally forgot they were coming. Terrible T. puts on his pants and opens the door after I get into the bedroom.

After we eat we're back at it again. Terrible T. is so sexual and for some reason I am more so than usual. He said he wanted to play a little game tonight since it's my last one in town. He tied my hands together and then to the headboard. He did the same thing to my feet and I am so turned on. Terrible T. leaves the room and comes back with a bandanna that he had in his coat pocket and ties my eyes shut. I feel so weird I love doing this but I have never had it done to me before. The next thing I know I can smell the candle that Jasmine put in the bathroom with me yesterday.

"Ouch!"

"Shh you will like this."

He did it again and since I was kinda expecting it didn't hurt as bad but it still burned. He began to suck on my nipples and I could feel how hard they were becoming. Terrible T. whispered in my ear, "JaLisa are you pregnant?"

"What? Why you ask me that?"

"Cause there is a little bit of milk coming out of your breast."

"What let me see, no it's not!"

He took the bandanna off and he was right but I know I'm not or at least I don't think I am pregnant. Why would milk be coming out of my nipples?

"I wish it was mine."

"You wish what was yours?"

"The baby, I wish it was mine."

"Ain't no baby Terrible T."

"Well why do you have milk coming out of your nipples then?"

"I don't know Terrible T.?"

He left me tied up but kept the bandanna off and started licking my piercing. I have a hundred and one thoughts going through my mind now and he is setting me into ecstasy with his mouth. What am I gonna tell Mama if I am pregnant and how in the hell did I let something like this happen. Richard is not ready to be a father. Richard, how am I going to tell Richard? He's out on tour and they want him to stay here in New York. I am so not ready to handle this with school and my job.

"Terrible T. please untie me I can't fully enjoy this while I am tied up."

"No, I'm keeping you here with me."

"Terrible T. don't be silly."

"I'm not being silly I really want you to stay and I want this to be my baby."

"There's no baby Terrible T."

"Okay but say you are pregnant, are you going to have it?"

"I can't even think about that right now."

He untied me and sat up on the bed. He lifted me off the bed and sat me on his lap and said, "I don't know what it is about you but you got me sprung."

"That's just lust Terrible T."

"Look JaLisa I am a grown man and I know my feelings I know how I feel and this right here just don't come and go. I really care about you and your well being that's why I did what I did today."

"I know Terrible T. and I appreciate everything you did for me today."

"No not that what I did for you was small."

"Then what do you mean Terrible T.?"

"I bought your boyfriend's contract from Something Else while you were getting massaged by Rosie."

"You did what?"

"Yeah I brought his contract for 1.8 million and he will get 1.3 of that it should already be in his account. I had my people work out all of the details."

"Terrible T. I don't understand, you can do something like that?"

"I pretty much can do anything I want JaLisa I am a very rich man."

"I don't know what to say. I mean I am so happy for Richard and I know this is what he always wanted. He talked so highly of you the last time I talked to him."

"So I will pretty much be his boss from here on out."

"Terrible T. this is crazy."

"I was suggesting that he gets a place here in New York."

"You mean you want him to leave Miami?"

"No, he can have a place in Miami but he's going to need to be here so often that he may be able to cut expenses if he has a place here as well."

"Damn Terrible T. this is a bit much to digest. You are telling me that my boyfriend is a millionaire and he's going to need to move to New York and that you're his boss. Anything else I should know?"

Terrible T. and I stayed up the rest of the night just talking about his world tours and how when he goes to other countries they are even more fascinated by him and his music than we are here in the United States. He promised that whatever happened between me and Richard that he still wanted to be a part of my life. When it came time for us to leave out to go to the airport we hugged and kissed and exchanged our goodbyes before we got to the car. Rashod and Jasmine rode with us so they wouldn't have to catch a cab. Terrible T. pulled into the garage at the airport so that he could go unnoticed. He told me to give him a few weeks and he was gonna make it his business to get down to Miami to see me even if it's only for a few hours.

On the plane Jasmine and I sat beside each other and Rashod sat on the opposite side of the aisle. We watched him doze off and Jasmine said, "So what are you gonna do?"

"About?"

"About . . . Terrible T. and Richard."

"Girl shit has got so out of control. I haven't been able to talk to you cause Terrible T. had me hostage but last night he told me that he brought Richard's contract."

"What?"

"Yes Bitch, Richard is a millionaire just like that."

"What do you mean?"

"Terrible T.'s company Def Jam brought Richard's contract from Something Else and Richard was given 1.3 million yesterday."

"Bitch are you jokin?"

"I'm dead f---in serious."

"Have you talked to Richard yet?"

"No, I had my phone turned off."

"Oh my God JaLisa you are rich."

"No Jasmine Richard is rich."

"Bitch please you know Richard gonna have you laced up."

"I'm so scared Jasmine."

"Why? What happened?"

"Last night Terrible T. was playin wit my nipples and milk came out."

"You're pregnant JaLisa!"

"I haven't taken a test yet."

"What the hell is wrong wit you? Milk in your titties means you pregnant. And you were throwin up for no reason the other night."

"I know I thought about that too."

"Damn JaLisa I don't know what to say."

"Girl my Mama's gonna kill me she can't stand Richard."

"She'll be able to stand him a whole lot betta once you tell her that he's rich."

"You think so?"

"Think girl money changes thangs didn't you know? Look at you . . . You look like a million bucks first thang in the morning with your diamond earrings, necklace and bracelet."

"I know I haven't been able to take them off since the ladies at the boutique put them on me."

"I'm so happy for you girl. Am I gonna be the God Mother?"

"We don't even know if I'm really pregnant and if I am I don't know if I'll be keeping it."

"Why, not?"

"Cause I . . . I mean I don't know if Richard is ready for the responsibility he's on tour now and he's gonna have to be in New York more."

"So you can go up there with him."

"Girl it's cold up there."

"JaLisa it's not cold up there all year round."

"Jasmine I don't even know if I want to tell him about me being pregnant if I am."

"Why?"

"Cause I don't want him to be distracted."

The Stewardess came around with a tray and something on there made me feel sick. I climbed over Jasmine and went into the bathroom it's so tight in here. I looked at myself in the mirror and my eyes started watering. I threw up everything I ate last night. I spit up all over the toilet lid and this time I had to clean the shit up myself. I do look good with all my new jewelry but my stomach is in a terrible condition. My breasts are so swollen and sore. Damn, I must really be pregnant and I don't know whether to laugh or cry. What was I thinkin sleepin wit Richard with no condoms? I used every paper towel in the little bathroom to clean up my mess. I tied the little trash bag into a knot then washed my hands and face before I came out.

When I came out the stewardess was waiting at the door.

She said, "Your friend told me that you are pregnant, congratulations."

"Well I don't know for sure yet but I guess thanks."

I handed her the bag of vomit since she wanted to be so happy for me and shit. When I got back to the seat again I climbed over Jasmine and said, "Don't tell anyone else I'm pregnant even when I confirm it I don't know how I'm going to handle this okay?"

"Okay but I still think you should be happy about all this JaLisa. Your life is about to totally change."

"How so?"

"Do you think Richard is gonna let his baby mama be broke?"

"Girl shut up!"

I don't even what to talk to Jasmine right now I have a million and one thoughts running through my mind. I'm sittin here staring out the window and picturing me and Richard in a huge house but not once have I seen a baby anywhere in the visual. I started to catch a chill so I waved the Stewardess down and she gave me a blanket. I wrapped up and dozed off and the next thing I knew we were told to put on out seatbelt because we would be landing in fifteen minutes.

~ RICHARD ~

The first thing I'm gonna do is buy JaLisa a new phone I have been calling her eva since I found out about this loot and I haven't been able to talk to her. That shit blows me. What if it was an emergency or something? I told Todd that I am gonna do the show tonight but this is my last night on the tour. It'll be Christmas in two days and I want to be home wit my baby. I booked a flight for first thang in the morning I am outta here until January. I called John and told him I had to go home and take care of some thangs and that I will be back in bout a week and he was cool wit that. I talked to Terrible T.'s assistant and she sounds more excited that I am. I let her know to tell Terrible T. that I will be back in a week and she told me that Terrible T. suggested to her that I should find a place up here because there will be a lot of traveling ova this coming year. I haven't even told JaLisa any thang I just hope she be down for a nigga. The last thang I want to do is mess my shit up wit her right now. I need her ass to keep me focused cause wit this Monica shit I was just wilding out. Speakin of Monica's ass she called me last night horny as hell and she had my d--- hard as a rock. She pulled one of JaLisa's moves and called me from the bath tub it was something about hearing that bath water that had me rock hard. I told her about the video that we did yesterday but I didn't mention the money. I don't want to tell no body about the money till I talk to JaLisa. Imma tell her she can quit that tired ass job and just go to school full-time if that's what she wants.

I don't want to put no pressure on her cause I know how she gets when she feels pressured. She starts trippin and shit. Back to Monica she asked was I gonna come see her and I said yeah. I think Imma go down there after I do this thang in New York next month. Then again wit all this loot I betta be careful cause who knows who's gonna be following me afta this shit. I told JT about the contract but I didn't mention shit about the money cause once a nigga find out got some shit going on they try to set you up. I don't wanna be all paranoid and shit but I gotta watch my back. The show ain't till tonight so I got the whole day to just chill. I picked up the phone to call the driver to tell him to come get a nigga out this room for a minute. He said he's gonna be here in an hour which will give me enough time to get my gear on.

I looked in the mirror and million or not I still look like the same nigga I did yesterday. I don't think the shit really hit me yet. When I turned the shower on I heard my cell ringing. It's JaLisa's house number.

"What's up baby?"

"It's okay I'm home today I didn't go to work."

"What's wrong you okay?"

"I wasn't feeling good my stomach hurts."

"Is it that time of month?"

"No, not yet."

"Then what's wrong baby?"

"I don't know Richard maybe something I ate. I called my job and left a message."

"You did baby?"

"Yeah, Richard when you coming home?"

"Real soon baby. I have a show tonight and this is my last night touring with the other Artist."

"Oh, yeah? What happened?"

"Something good happened baby just like I told you but I don't want to talk to you about it on the phone. I want to be looking into your eyes when I tell you how lucky we've just become."

JaLisa told me to hold on and I could hear her throwin up. Damn she sounds bad. She might have food poisoning or some shit.

"Richard, are you still there?"

"I'm still here baby. Maybe you should go to the emergency room."

"I'll be okay I have just been ripping and running and I need to get a day of sleep."

"Okay baby if you say so. I'm gonna be at Ft. Lauderdale at 9 o'clock in the morning. Can you pick me up?"

"Of course I'll pick you up. I thought you wasn't gonna be here for Christmas."

"I'm coming home for you beautiful."

"Okay baby I'll be there."

"Alright get some rest so you can have enough energy for me to tomorrow."

"I will baby."

There's steam and shit all ova my room. I had the hot water in the shower running while I was on the phone. Damn I hope my baby is okay. She didn't sound good at all. I never heard her throw up before. That shit sounds gross. I jump in and out the shower, dressed and was down stairs waiting for the driver when he pulled up.

"Where to Richard?" The driver asked.

"A jewelry store I need to buy a diamond ring."

"What? You poppin the question?"

"Yeah as soon as I get back to Miami."

"She's going to be so surprised."

"Yeah jus bout errythang I'm gonna tell her."

"How much you want to spend?"

"What?"

"How much you want to spend that way I can know where to take you?"

"I'mma spend 10 g's on my baby."

"Cool let's go to Jacob the Jeweler. He has some of the best shit in town."

"You the driva."

We got to Jacob the Jeweler in bout ten minutes and parked right out front. I hopped out and the driver came in wit me. He pressed the doorbell to get in and this young chick came and opened the door for us. I couldn't tell where she's from but I know she ain't from here. She looked me up and down and said what can I do for you. I said, "I wanna buy my girl a ring."

She said, "My uncle ain't here but I'm sure I can help you find a ring. He won't be back till 4 o'clock."

She let us in and locked the door back. When I say they have some shit up in here I mean they have some shit up in here. I seen some shit I want for myself but that's gonna have to be on the next visit. I pulled out all the money I got for doing that opening show for Terrible T. and laid it on the counter so she would know that I mean business. I told her that it was 10 g's. She said, "I'm not gonna even ask where you got all this money from."

I said, "And I ain't gonna tell you either."

She showed me what she licked and told me to describe JaLisa to her.

"JaLisa has a coconut brown complexion. She likes to wear long braids but she has her own hair it comes down to her shoulders. She has one of the most beautiful smiles I have eva seen in my life. She's about 5'7 wit a small waist and a phat ass."

She started blushing when I said that. She said, "Sounds like you love this JaLisa."

"I wouldn't be in here if I didn't."

She showed me this 4-carat Marquise cut diamond ring and I was like that's it. That's the ring. I know exactly what JaLisa likes I know she is gonna love this one.

She said, "This one is more that ten thousand dollars but I am going to let you take it for that since you have cash. I don't think my uncle will mind you just have to promise to come back and give us more business."

"Yo, you got my word on that there."

I looked at the driver and he gave me the nod ov approval. She cleaned the ring wit something out of this pink bottle and put the ring in a ring box. I took the box and stuck it in my pocket. She gave me a receipt and said, "As long as it's not damaged you can bring it back if JaLisa doesn't want it."

"I don't think I will have that problem. She's gonna love this ring."

She came from behind the counter and let us out and locked the door behind us.

The driver said, "Where to next?"

"I'm all spent out. The rest of my loot is in the bank and I ain't tryin to go hit that up just yet."

~ JALISA ~

I've been in the bed since I got home. If this is what pregnant feels like I don't want no parts of it. I finally got up to empty the trash can beside my bed and put something on to go to the CVS Pharmacy down the street. When I walked inside the Pharmacy my head started spinning. This is the final hour I'm about to find out my fate. So I walk to aisle 10A and there they are, in every brand that you can think of. I chose the one that tells you PREGNANT or NOT PREGNANT it's new I saw it on a commercial last week but I never imagined that I would be needing one for myself. The weird thing is that I haven't missed a period that's why I don't think I really am. Maybe my nerves are just bad that's why I'm so sick. When I get to the check out there is a problem cause the box won't scan. The young ass hole behind the counter announces to the world.

"I need a price check on a Precisely Right Pregnancy Test."

He not only says it once but he's at it again.

"I need a price check on a Precisely Right Pregnancy Test."

I say, "It's twenty-five dollars dammit."

"Sorry Ma'am but it's not scanning so I need a new box."

Just as I was bout to smack his ass wit the test his Manager came from behind the glass wall and told him to punch in the numbers instead of swiping it across the scanner. When he did I found out that it was on sale for seven-teen dollars. I gave him a twenty and snatched the change out of his hand.

When I got back to the house I ran to the bathroom and peed on the stick and sat the test on the side of the sink. I didn't even want to look at it so I walked outta the bathroom to the kitchen and poured myself some grapefruit juice. I would love to have some Vodka but not before I find out the results. I took a drink from the cup and sat it on the counter. When I got back to the bathroom the test was already finished. P R E G N A N T is what it read and I burst out crying. What am I going to do wit a baby? I cried so much that I started throwin up all ova again. Well I don't have to go back to work for another three days cause tomorrow is Christmas Eve so that gives me a couple of more days to get myself together.

It just dawned on me that I haven't brought anything for Mama or Richard and he's coming back tomorrow. When I called him earlier I was feeling sick but I wanted to hear his voice. He told me to pick him up in the morning. I feel so bad cause I already know this good news he wants to tell me about and I really don't want to tell him my news at all. Who says he has to know.

Afta I washed my face I went to the closet to find the Yellow Pages. I found the page with the Women Center's on it and I pick up the cordless phone to dial the one in Kendall and it rings in my hand.

"Hello."

"Hey girl you okay? You didn't look so hot when we got off the plane."

"Yeah I'm okay. I was just about to call the Women's Center in Kendall."

"So you took a test?"

"Yeah I went to the CVS down the street earlier."

"So what are you going to do?"

"Didn't I just say I was calling the Women's Center? What do you think I'm gonna do?"

"But JaLisa be reasonable you haven't even told Richard yet have you?"

"No, and I don't plan to. I'm picking him up tomorrow from Ft. Lauderdale and I told him I may have food poisoning."

"JaLisa what did I tell you about lying it's never good cause you have to keep up wit them."

"Look Jasmine he's about to come home tomorrow and tell me that he's a millionaire I am not about to hit him wit no Baby MaMa drama."

"JaLisa you not thinkin straight right now. Please don't do something that you may regret the rest of your life. Have you talked to your Mama yet?"

"Hell No!"

"Have you told her that you're back in town?"

"Didn't I just say that I ain't talked to my Mama!"

"Okay enough of that, you gonna do what you wanna do anyway."

"You right about that."

"So what you doing the rest of the day?"

"Not shit why you ask?"

"Cause I need to buy my Mama and Rashod some Christmas gifts and I wanted to ride out to Sawgrass Mills Mall."

"I guess I'll pick you up in bout an hour I need to get myself together that mall is big as shit."

"Okay just call me when you leavin the house."

"Cool."

Jasmine gets on my f----- nerves sometimes always up in my business. I bet she dun told her Mama and them already that I'm pregnant. She lucky I need to get my Mama and Richard something for Christmas cause I would not be going out to no damn Sawgrass Mills Mall. That shit too big and I ain't in the mood for all that walkin. I called the Women's Center anyway just to find out how much it was gonna cost to get this ova wit. Some cheery bitch answers the phone.

"Good Afternoon this is the Women's Center of Kendall how may I direct your call?"

"Yes, I wanted to know the price of a . . ."

"It's okay dear it depends on how far you are?"

"I don't know cause I've still been getting my periods on time."

"That's okay you will need to come in and be examined before we can determine a price."

"So what's your first available appointment?"

"Well since it's the holiday's we won't be back open till the 27th."

"That's four days away!"

"Yes it is, would like to schedule an appointment at this time?"

"That's too many days to be here thinkin."

"Excuse me, I'm sorry I didn't hear you."

"Never mind I'll call back."

"Okay dear I wish you luck."

"Yeah uh huh thanks, bye."

I threw the phone book back in the closet and turned on the shower. I feel so sticky. The weather here is so different from New York. It's like 80 degrees here today and 20 degrees in New York."

Before I could get in the shower my cell rings and it's Terrible T.

"Hi Terrible T. how are you?"

"Thinking about you."

"I was jus thinkin about you too and the weather up there. It's in the 80's here."

"Don't remind me. How are you feeling?"

"I'm doing a little better I have thrown up in like an hour."

"So did you find out?"

"Yeah, I am?"

"Wow! Did you tell him yet?"

"No he doesn't know."

"I'll be down there to see you in two weeks I've already set it up for your boy to be here in New York working on a project."

"Okay Terrible T."

"I don't want you down there being all down and shit. Is it anything you need?"

"No Terrible T., you've done so much."

"I can't stop thinkin bout you, and you being here."

"I know me too."

"Hold on a minute alright."

Someone walked into the room and I could hear him talking to them. He came back to the phone and said, "Okay baby I'll call you back a little later to check on you."

"Okay Terrible T. talk to you later."

I hung up the phone and plugged it up to charge so my battery won't run out while we're at the mall. It feels so good to be in my own shower. That hotel shower was the bomb but it's nothing like being home where everything is familiar. I stood in the shower and let the water run all ova my back and I turned around to the front. I rubbed the soap over my breasts and they are so tender. I can't be just one month feeling like this. I take the soap and rub my belly. I just thought I had picked up a few pounds when I had trouble getting into some of my clothes. As I rubbed the soap ova my belly it felt like it fluttered. My heart jumped and I'm in here crying again. I'm not ready for this. I let the water wash the soap and the tears away and I turned the water off and stepped out the shower.

When I looked at myself in the mirror I can hardly recognize myself from earlier today. The jewelry that Terrible T. brought me I took it off when I got home and wrapped it up and put it in the back of my closet where the money that Richard gave me is. I went back to the money that Richard gave me and took it all out of the box and put into my little black purse that I'm gonna carry to the mall. I'm wearing my tan Capri pants today with a sleeveless white top and my comfortable shoes that I brought a few months back from Barefeet Shoe Store. These shoes feel like I'm walking on pillows.

I feel a little better after the shower and my stomach is feeling hungry but I don't want to eat because I'll be sick at the mall. I stuffed my lip gloss in my purse with the money and my ID and I'm on my way to pick up Jasmine and she better not start wit that shit cause I will happily turn right back around and come home. I called her from my cell so that she would be ready by the time I get there. When I pulled up she's down stairs and we are off to the Highway. It takes like forty-five minutes to get there from Jasmines house. She gets into the car all chipper.

"Hey how are you feeling?"

"Better since I took a shower."

"Yeah you look refreshed."

"Thanks but I need to take out these braids."

"Why they still look good to me."

"I just don't feel like being bothered with them any more I want to see my own hair."

"I know what you mean that's why I don't really like to get braids."

One of Miz Thang' songs "You and I" came on the radio and all I could think about is Terrible T. Jasmine started laughing she said, "I know who you thinkin bout."

"Girl he called me before I was about to jump in the shower."

"Really, what did he say?"

"He was just asking me how I was feeling and that he would be down here in two weeks. He said that he was gonna make sure that Richard would be New York."

"JaLisa this is so exciting."

"For who?"

"Bitch you can't tell me that you are not excited about all this."

"Well I guess. I would probably be more excited if I felt better."

"I understand."

The rest of the ride we rode in silence. When we got there I wanted to park outside the mall instead of the garage. I want to feel the warm sun against my skin. I really missed Miami and I'm so glad to be home. I don't know if I will be able to stand New York for too long. It's too cold for one and the people walk so fast. Where in the hell are they in such a hurry to get to. Then again if it were cold like that here I would be walking just as fast. Jasmine interrupted my thoughts with, "So what store are we going in first?"

"It's on you."

"Well my Mama already told me that she wants a cell phone so that will be easy. We can just go to the Metro PCS store cause she never leaves Miami."

"I didn't even ask my Mama what she wanted."

We walked pass a baby store and we both saw a mother breast feeding a newborn baby right out in the open on the bench.

"See that ain't gon be me."

"Why not JaLisa they say that breast milk is the best milk?"

"Do you have any kids?"

"Okay, well, have some of your own and you can put your titties all in their mouth."

"Girl you're a trip."

"No I ain't a trip I'm real."

We passed by the Cinnamon Bun Shop and I swear they were calling my name from behind the counter. I ordered an extra large bun with extra icing.

"Girl you gon get sick again from all that icing."

"Well I just have to be sick then cause I want this here."

We found the Metro PCS store and Jasmine got her Mama a cell phone with unlimited local and long distance calling. I went on and got my Mama one also just cause she needs one when she at the grocery store and just out by herself. I brought Richard two platinum money clips and got his name engraved on them for all that cash he's gonna have in his pockets. I also brought him some Marc Jacobs cologne for men I brought the biggest one I could find. It feels like the life has been sucked out of me and I am ready to go home now.

"You ready to go?" I asked Jasmine.

"I'm ready when you are."

"Good let's roll."

~ RICHARD ~

I have about an hour before the driver comes to pick us up for the show tonight. We have to be there early to do a sound check. When I got back from the jeweler earlier I asked the front desk attendant to give me the key to the safe that's in my room so that I could lock JaLisa's ring up. I went ahead and packed up my stuff too so that I will be ready to leave in the morning. Ain't no telling what time we will get back here tonight with the after parties and shit.

I told JT I was going back home tomorrow for a week and I'm droppin the tour and he said that he's out too. He said he was gonna spend bout a week in Atlanta wit Resha' before he went home. Of course he's trippin but I ain't gon be the nigga to tell him how twisted he sounds. I've been going over my music since I been back in my room cause tonight's gonna be big. I'll be able to promote my solo shit. Who knows who'll show up tonight? When I talked to Todd earlier he said for me to be on my toes cause he thinks Terrible T. might send some of his people ova. He also told me that my first video gon air New Year's Eve. They gon play it before the ball drops. All I can say is I'm brining in the New Year real big. Doing real big thangs.

~ JALISA ~

I made Jasmine drive back to her house and I leaned my seat back and dozed off. I had a vision of Terrible T. he spoiled me in a big way this week and now I don't want to do nothing. I sure as hell don't want to go back to that tired ass job but I know I have to stick with school. I don't care if Richard has money or not I still need my education. I don't want to be caught up in a statistic. I woke back up when Jasmine put on the Yolanda Adams CD that I had in the car from when I went to work last week. She keeps repeating the song "In the Midst of it all." She sings, "not because I've been faithful, not because I've always obeyed, it's not because I trust Him, to be with me all of the way, but it's because he loves me so dearly." I know I ain't all spiritual but I do believe in God no matter how I may cut up. I know that He wouldn't put more on me than I can put up with. I can't wait till the day when I can give Brenda Hicks my notice. I don't even want to see the expression on her face. I'm gonna have to send her an email or something cause I'll probably get cursed out real good. Especially when I tell her about Richard's million-dollar contract and just think she has a problem wit my man. I'll bet she will never meet any man as half as good as Richard has been to me.

Jasmine pulls up in front of her house and turns on the inside light. She say, "You betta go home and get some rest cause you know you have to be at the Airport in the morning."

"I know, I am if I wasn't picking Richard up I would just let you drive me home."

"You want me to come home wit you? All I have to do is put this stuff in the house and grab me some clothes you can just drop me off in the morning."

99

"No, I don't want you to put yourself out there like that."

"Girl stop tripping you my best friend just wait right here I'll run in the house. I'll be five minutes."

While Jasmine was in the house my eyes and mouth started watering again. I open the passenger side door and threw up that entire Cinnamon bun I had at the mall. My throat is starting to burn. I didn't chew the bun up enough cause I can feel every lump coming back up. This shit is so gross. I have to do something about this real fast. Jasmine came out the house and sees me. She ran back in the house and got me some cold wet paper towels to wipe my face and put ova my head.

"Thanks Jasmine girl if I'm like this in the morning I ain't gon be able to drive out to Ft. Lauderdale."

"Don't worry bout that I'll pick Richard up."

"You'd to that?"

"I love you JaLisa you my best friend I'd do any thang for you girl."

Jasmine stopped at the gas station to fill the car up and get me a Ginger Ale before we got back to my house. She carried my bags out the car and unlocked the door for me. When I got in all I could smell was those damn Glad Plug In's and any other time I would love them but that shit is makin me want to throw up again. I run to the bathroom and threw up the lining of my stomach. I'm in so much pain that this shit just can't be healthy. I closed the door cause I didn't want Jasmine looking at me from the doorway. There's blood in the toilet as I continue to vomit.

"Lord help me! I can't take this no more."

When I'm finally finished I flush the toilet and was my face and hands. The only thing I want to do is get into the bed. When I get to my bedroom Jasmine is sitting on my bed and she has one of Richard's big T-shirts spread out for me to put on. I took off everything right in front of her and put the T-shirt on. She's staring at me and then she starts to cry.

I said, "What the hell you cryin for? I'm the one should be crying."

"I love you JaLisa and I hate seeing you hurting like this."

"I'll be okay Jasmine."

I sat beside her on the bed then I thought of how bad my breath smelt and I went to go brush my teeth. When I came back in the room she was sitting there with her head in her hands crying very softly. I sat beside her again on the bed and wrapped my arm around her.

I said, "I'll be okay Jasmine don't worry about me."

She put both her hands on my face and started kissing me and I closed my eyes and kissed her back. What the hell are we doing? We ain't gay but this feels so natural.

She said, "I'm sorry but I've been wanting to do that for a long time."

"What?"

"Yes but don't be mad at me."

"I ain't mad at you."

We both closed our eyes and kissed again this time it was so sensual. I've never imagined kissing a woman before especially not my best friend. She started kissing my neck and even though my stomach hurts like hell I really would like to see how far she's gonna go with this. If I stop her I know how she is and I will hurt her feelings real bad. But if I let her keep going it may ruin what we have built for years. She has her eyes closed and she's kissing me her lips feel so soft and I totally can't believe this is happening right now of all times. Jasmine laid me back on the bed and she licked my nipples and started massaging my breasts. Her hands are so soft. She's actually rubbing on my clit and comes to my ring.

"You never told me you had this."

"Girl I don't tell you everything. I never thought you would be interested in hearing about it."

She moves from my breasts and kisses my stomach. She's laying her head softly on my stomach.

She says, "If you decide to have the baby I'll help you take care of it."

"What you talkin bout Jasmine."

"I'm serious I'll help you."

"I don't have any doubt about that but that's not what I want."

"What do you want JaLisa. Do you even know?"

Before I could answer she was sucking on my clit. I don't believe this shit. Her mouth is so warm. Oh my goodness. What is really going on?

"Jasmine what are you doing."

She doesn't answer but she sure knows what she's doing.

"Where did you learn that from . . . have you been with a woman before Jasmine?"

"I don't tell you everything; remember what you said about the piercing."

She's not wild like Richard nor is she as good as Terrible T. but on a scale of 1-10 she is definitely up there. She's rolling her tongue around my clit and I really don't believe this at all. I guess we all have secrets. I pray this doesn't mess up our beautiful friendship.

"Jasmine, why are you doing this?"

"Cause I've always wanted to since high school but I didn't want you to think differently about me."

"You know you could have talked to me about anything."

She wipes her mouth on my blanket and kisses me again. I closed my eyes and don't know where my mind is wondering to or why we are even doing this but it feels so different. I like the way she kisses. She doesn't try to take ova my entire mouth. I am so moist right now. She goes from my neck back down to my breasts and her hands feel so soft. Richard would kill me if he found out this shit but not Terrible T. this would totally turn him on. He'd probably sit back drinking Cristal and just watch. She's sucking on me again and I couldn't help but hold her head in place cause she just reached my spot and has me cumming so softly. Jasmine went and got my wash cloth and wiped my mouth then she wiped me off, pulled the T-shirt down and put the covers over me.

When she came back from the bathroom I was turned facing the wall. She came and lay behind me and just held me the rest of the night.

She whispered in my ear, "Are you okay with what just happened?"

"Yes, Jasmine you made me feel so good."

"Do you want me to leave?"

"No, I don't want to be alone tonight."

"Is this gonna change things."

"Not if you don't want it to."

"I'm sorry JaLisa I just hate to see you feeling so bad."

"It's okay Jasmine trust me. It's okay."

I rolled over and even though it's dark in here I can clearly see her face. I kissed her and I could still taste myself on them. She closed her eyes and I could feel her breath. I reached behind her back and unhooked her bra. I took my hand and rubbed her skin until I was holding one of her breasts. Her breathing is getting deeper. As I made circles around her nipples with my tongue I slid off her panties. I pulled the covers up over my head and made my way down to her clit and gave her what she had just given me. She's moaning my name and all I can think of is I wish Terrible T. was here to give us both some d---. She is holding the covers so tight and moving all around so I must be doing it right. I never imagined I would be doing this to any woman especially not my best friend.

"Oh JaLisa, thank you."

Eventually I could feel her cumming she took her thighs and squeezed my head so tight. Her skin is so soft. After she cums I keep licking her until she can't take anymore and pushes my head away.

"I love you JaLisa."

"I love you to Jasmine."

I get up and get her a wash cloth from the closet. This time I wipe her off by the time I got back from the bathroom with the warm wash cloth she's asleep. I went back to the bathroom to brush my teeth again and climb in the bed next to her. This time I held her and fall asleep.

When I wake up Jasmine is gone and I look around my room like I was dreaming. Was she here last night? That was some of best sleep I have had in a very long time. I get up look to out the window and the car is gone and there's a note on the table.

You looked so sweet sleeping that I didn't bother to wake you.
I'll be back soon with your boy friend.

Luv Jasmine

~ RICHARD ~

When I got off the plane I went to get my bags and Jasmine is standing there waiting for me.

She said, "I had to come get you cause JaLisa got real sick last night."

"I wonder what's wrong wit her I told her to go to the hospital yesterday but she said she was gonna be alright."

"I told her too but she just won't listen."

"Thanks fo cumming to scoop a nigga."

"No problem anything for JaLisa."

I grabbed my bags and we went get the car. I took Jasmine home she said that she had some things to do this morning and she would holla at JaLisa a little later. She asked me a hundred questions about the tour and Terrible T. I was bout ready to get her out the car when I pulled up to her crib.

She said, "Tell my girl I'll call her later to check up."

"Cool."

Before I got to JaLisa's I saw one of those people selling roses on the side of the road and I got her some white ones. I think she'll like these. I slid through the corner store and got her a two-liter Ginger Ale and a box of crackers. When I get to her house she is standing in the doorway looking like an Angel. First thang in the morning and all she's still beautiful. I don't know weather its cause my T-shirt so big on her or not but her breasts look big as shit. I jumped out the car and left all the shit I had jus brought and snatched her up. I feel like a nigga jus coming from the army or some shit. Damn I missed my baby. We kissed and of course my d--- got hard as shit.

She said, "Well I know one of you is happy to see me."

I asked her, "So you feel any betta?"

"Yeah a little."

I left back out the door to go get the flowers and stuff I got from the store. I put the bag down and pulled the little box out my pocket I can't wait. I got down on one knee like a real nigga do and asked her, "JaLisa will you marry me?"

When she saw that rock she started crying like a baby. She said, "Are you sure you want to do this?"

"Hell yeah I'm sure I don't ever want to be wit out you girl. I missed you like shit when I was in New York."

I'm still on the floor and she's hugging me around my head.

She said, "Of course I will marry you Richard."

I got up and picked her up and carried her to the room. I know my d--- is hard as shit but I ain't bout to make love to her till she feel betta. She kissed me on the lips as I laid her across the bed.

I said, "I have some good news baby."

"Oh yeah?"

"Yeah, look Terrible T. brought my contract for ova a million dollars and it's all ours baby."

"Are you serious that's amazing Richard!"

She squeezed my head between her breast and they do seem bigger than I remember. I just wanna grab one of em but I know she's not feeling good. When I told her about the money she didn't get as excited as I thought she would but I guess cause she's not feeling well.

"Do you like the ring?"

"I love my ring!"

"I got it from this place named Jacob the Jeweler."

"All the rappers talk about this place, thank you baby I really love it."

"So what are we doing for Christmas?"

"I have to go to spend some time with Mama and you can come with me."

"Yo Mama don't like me JaLisa."

"She will especially when she see that you are serious about me."

"A'aight."

"I love the roses Richard white is my favorite."

"I'm glad I can put a smile on your face."

"Richard."

"Yeah babe what's up?"

She got up off the bed and walked ova to me and sat on my lap. She hugged me so tight around my neck and we kissed. She closed her eyes and laid her head on my shoulder. It feels so good just to hold her in my arms again.

"Richard are you gonna move to New York?"

"Well it may be smart for me to get a little place there just cause it would come out cheaper than staying in a hotel every time I have to go up there."

"So what does that mean for us?"

"It means I want you as my wife and I wanna spend the rest of my life wit you."

"But I don't wanna live in New York."

"You don't have to move there baby but when I have to go away for weeks at a time I'm gonna want you to come spend time wit me."

"And I will."

"After Christmas I'm gonna transfer some money to your account so I'll need your bank info."

"Okay baby."

"Is there anything you wanna talk to me about?"

"No, why you say that Richard?"

"Just the expression on your face that's all."

"What expression?"

"Don't worry about it just forget it."

JaLisa got up and walked towards the bathroom and she came back holding something white in her hand.

She said, "I do have something to tell you."

"What up? What's that you got?"

She gave me this little white stick that read PREGNANT. I looked at the stick and looked up at her and she's crying.

"So this is why you been sick but I thought you said you came on?"

"I did."

"Then you need to go to the doctors JaLisa cause you need to make sure that you alright."

"Okay I will."

I scooped her up off the floor and held her as tight as I could.

"So you know how far you are?"

"No, not yet."

"I'm so happy baby it's all coming together."

~ JALISA ~

Richard's back, he's in my room sleeping like a baby and its only noon. He said that he didn't get a lot of sleep in New York. I went on told him about the baby just because I felt he had the right to know. That still doesn't mean that I'm keeping it but at least he knows. My cell rings and I grab it before it can wake up Richard. It's Jasmine's house number.

"What's up girl?" I say in a whisper.

I walk to the back and close my bedroom door and head to the kitchen.

"Ain't shit, where's your boyfriend?"

"You mean, my fiancée."

"What?"

"Yeah girl he gave me this big ass 4-Carat ring that he got from Jacob the Jeweler in New York."

"And you said yes?"

"Yeah why not I love him?"

"Did you tell him about the baby?"

Yes, I did and he's very happy."

"Well that's good, so that means your having the baby?"

"No, I didn't say all that."

"Okay smart ass."

"I'm not trying to be smart Jasmine I just don't know what I'm gonna do right now. He talking about he go be wanting me to come to New York and he gon have to get a place up there. Shit I don't know what's gonna happen but I do know one thing I have a 4-Carat rock on my finger today and that makes me very happy."

"Oh I see."

"Good I'm glad you do."

"Have you been thinking about last night?"

"Girl I've been so occupied with Richard I haven't thought about anything."

"Oh."

"I can tell you one thing."

"What's that?"

"It was very different."

"What do you mean by that?"

"Jasmine I've never been wit a woman before and to have my first experience with my best friend was very different."

"So what are you gonna do?"

"About . . . What? Jasmine."

"Never mind JaLisa look my mom is bugging me about something I'll call you back later."

"Okay talk to you later."

I don't know what the hell Jasmine is getting at but what we did last night needs not to happen again. Why the hell is everybody all ways asking what am I gonna do. Shit I don't even know what I'm gonna do. I feel like pulling these damn braids out. As a matter of fact that's exactly what I'm gonna do. I turned the TV on to E! True Hollywood Stories and started from the back of my head taking these damn braids out.

It's a miracle I didn't throw up today so that must be a good sign. I was starting to think something wasn't right. The house phone rings and it's so loud I know it had to wake Richard. It's my Mama.

"Hey Mama how is everything?"

"Everything is good baby. I just haven't heard from you in a few days and that's not like you at JaLisa."

"I know Mama but I have been so busy with school and work and just everything."

"Too busy for your Mama baby?"

"No Mama I'm never too busy for you I just . . . well I don't really have an excuse."

"Good no excuses so what time should I expect to see you tomorrow?"

"I'll be there about 1 o'clock Mama I want to sleep in tomorrow."

"Okay baby that's fine just bring an appetite cause you know I'm cookin up some stuff over her."

"I know I will. Mama I'm bringing Richard tomorrow is that okay?"

"Well I was kinda expecting it would just be me and you like always but I guess one more won't hurt."

"Mama."

"Yes baby is everything alright?"

"Everything is just fine we'll see you tomorrow. Love you."

"Love you too baby I'll see you tomorrow."

Richard came out the room I knew the phone woke him up.

"I told Mama we would be there at about 1 o'clock tomorrow."

"What did she say?"

"It's cool baby."

"If you say so, what are you doing?"

"Taking out my braids wanna help?"

Richard sat behind me on the couch and helped me take out my braids we watched E! True Hollywood Stories they are doing a special on Sammy Davis Jr. It's great how he opened the doors for so many black people around the world. I had no idea he was a part of the "Rat Pack" with Frank Sinatra.

"You know Richard, I've been thinking if you are gonna be spending a lot of time traveling it's no reason for us to have two places here in Miami. How would you feel moving your things in here? You know I have the extra bedroom and whatever can't fit in here you can either put it in storage or give it to someone who needs it."

He kissed me on the back of my neck and said, "JaLisa that's cool I knew we would figure this thang out."

~ RICHARD ~

I didn't realize how tired I was until I laid across JaLisa's bed. The phone woke me up it was her Mama we going ova there for Christmas tomorrow. I sure hope her Mama don't be trippin and shit especially since she's pregnant. She had me taking out her braids the rest of the night. My arms are so tired as shit but I know she wanted a nigga's help or she wouldn't have asked. That's just how she is. While I'm helping her wit her braids we watching E! True Hollywood Stories and all I could think about was that damn Monica. I had to turn my cell phone off cause she called earlier but JaLisa was in the bathroom. That's the last thang I need right now while shit going good. My d--- is hard as shit thinking about Monica's red ass. JaLisa asked was I hard for her and of course I had to lie she just wouldn't understand.

When she told me about the baby I was in shock. Not that I don't want a baby but I've neva got nobody pregnant before and I know there's a lot of time involved that I'm not gonna be about to give with me traveling and shit. On Monday Imma put 100 g's in Jalisa's account and that should hold her for a minute. I want her to quit that tired ass job and focus on school like she wants to do.

Afta she took those braids out she jumped in the shower and came out looking like a different person. Her hair is wet and curly and hanging down to her shoulders and she's got me harder than a Mutha f----. She didn't even dry off before I grabbed her and slobbed her down. She has a little pouch forming at the bottom of her stomach and her breasts are sitting up on her chest. I laid her down on the bed and sucked her like she was my wife.

"Richard slow down baby my stomach."

I stopped sucking for a minute and held both her breasts in my hand. It looks like she's had her boobs done. Before I could do anything else to her she turns me ova and unbuttons my pants and slides them to the floor. She ain't even take off my boxers she just pulled him out and went to town.

"You missed a nigga huh?"

"Yeah, I did."

I don't know why Monica keeps poppin in my head but I'm picturing the first time she went down on me by the window in my hotel room.

"Oh shit JaLisa!"

Before I knew what was happening she drank a nigga dry. I didn't want that to happen but her mouth felt so good. She came up and kissed me on my lips and laid beside me on the bed. She just wanted me to hold her and I'm cool wit that. I pulled her close to me and put my hand on her stomach. I could feel her body tense and then she relaxed in my arms. I really missed this while I was in New York.

~ JaLisa ~

Its Christmas morning and I have been throwing up since 5AM. Richard is asleep and has no idea that I'm in the bathroom again. I feel so weak I don't know what's left in my stomach. I throw up one last time and again I throw up blood. My stomach must be under so much stress that it's bleeding. I stable myself on the toilet so that I can stand to my feet and I fall back on the floor. My head hits the side of the toilet as I fall. Richard heard the loud noise and bust into the bathroom. Before I can flush the toilet he sees the blood and goes off.

"What the hell is going on JaLisa why are you throwing up blood?"

"I don't know!"

"What just happened did you fall on the floor?"

"Yes."

"I'm calling the ambulance right now!"

"No, Richard please I'm okay."

"JaLisa yo ass ain't okay. How long have you been throwing up blood?"

"For about three days."

He pulls me up off the floor and carries me to the bedroom. He goes to my closet and finds a pair of my workout pants and put them on me. He puts one of his T-shirts on me and slides my feet into my flip-flops. As we walk to the car I almost pass out again I feel so weak. Richard is driving like a bat outta hell we pull up in front of Memorial West Regional Hospital and he parks. He goes straight to the check in desk and says she's bleeding and she pregnant. The lady at the desk grabs the nurse and they take me to the back in a wheel chair. I feel so faint. Richard picked me up out the wheel chair and sat me on the hospital bed. By this time there is blood all ova my pants. I can feel these sharp pains in my stomach and I started screaming.

"Richard I'm losing the baby!"

He's crying I've never seen Richard cry before. The doctor came ova and told the nurse to hook me up to the monitors so that they could hear the baby's heart beat. There's nothing there. The doctor asked how long have you been throwing up blood.

Richard answers, "She told me it's been three days doctor."

"You should have come to the emergency then."

The nurse hooked me up to an IV and stuck a needle in it the next thing I knew I was dozing off.

When I finally woke up Mama and Richard was standing ova my bed and I had my own room. Mama was crying and telling me she had a dream about fish last week but she didn't tell me about it. It's Christmas day and we are all in the hospital. Richard said he called Jasmine and she was crying and screaming in the phone. He told her that they would be releasing me soon so she could just come see me at the house. Mama held my hand and she said, "I wish you would have talked to me baby."

"I know Mama please forgive me."

"Its okay baby Richard told me about the record deal and how he's going to be back and forth to New York."

"He did."

"Yes when he called me I couldn't think so he said he would come pick me up and we were talking on the way here and while they were giving you some time to rest."

"Oh."

Richard said, "I'm gonna leave you two for a minute."

"Okay baby."

He kissed me on my forehead and I could see the hurt in his eyes.

"JaLisa the doctor said that you were four months pregnant and since you didn't know that you didn't take care of yourself like you should have. He said that you probably would not be able to have kids again."

"Oh Mama!" I cried.

"No baby it's gonna be okay the doctor said that when you are ready to have a baby there are a series of operations that you could go through and that may work."

"What have I done?"

"What do you mean baby you didn't know?"

"But Mama I kept saying that I didn't want the baby."

~ RICHARD ~

I don't know what the hell is going on one minute I'm holding JaLisa in my arms the next she's in the bathroom throwing up blood. The doctor said that she was four months pregnant with my little boy. You wanna see a grown man cry and feel hopeless jus tell him that he's lost his only chance to reproduce. The doctor said that my soon to be wife may not ever be able to have children again and I don't know how to digest that. My parents which were my only family was killed in a plane crash three years ago coming from Jamaica in a storm. That was the last time I remember crying. I had them both cremated because I couldn't stand the fact that if they would have been in the ground with no head stones. I still have the ashes in my apartment. My cell rings while I'm in the waiting area. I left JaLisa and her mom alone to talk.

"Hello."

"Hi sexy, Merry Christmas, I just wanted to hear your voice how are you?"

"Not so good."

"What's wrong Santa didn't bring you no gifts?"

"No, JaLisa jus lost our baby."

"Oh my God Richard I'm so sorry."

"Yeah me too."

"You gonna be okay baby. Is there anything I can do?"

"Nah I jus have to be here for her she depressed as hell."

"I'm sure she is. I'm so sorry Richard."

"Look I have to go."

I hung up the phone and I'm crying again. JaLisa's mom is walking towards me she comes and put her arm around me.

She says, "Baby it's gonna be okay. The Lord does everything for a reason and we don't know why he took our little baby but at least we know that now he's a little angel."

"Yes Ma'am your right. I believe that."

"Look Richard I know we had a rocky start but I need you to be strong for my little girl. She's gonna need you right now or at least until you have to go back out of town then I'll step in."

"Yes Ma'am you've got my word."

She grabbed my face and kissed me on the cheek and told me that I should go in and talk to JaLisa before I take her home. When I got in the room JaLisa was staring out the window crying. I leaned over and kissed her on the forehead.

"Baby I'm so sorry."

She didn't respond she just stared out the window. I have never seen her like this. I don't know what to say to her to make things better.

"Baby it's not . . . baby it's gonna be okay."

She just blinked the tears out her eyes and she closed them. The medicine must be makin her drowsy. The doctor walked in the room and wrote out three prescriptions on for pain, another for an antibiotic and the last he said is for depression.

The doctor said, "Okay JaLisa I am going to release you now I need you to take all of your medication and follow up with your Primary Care Physician in one week. If you start to have uncontrollable vaginal bleeding please don't hesitate to come to the Emergency room."

The doctor signaled for me to come to the hall with him and said, "I'm releasing her because it's nothing else we can do for her and sometimes it's better if the patient can go back to their own environment to recover. JaLisa is real depressed and she blames herself for what happened so I'm going to need you to watch her and make sure she takes her medication it will make her better in a few days."

"You got it doc, thanks for everything."

The nurse helped JaLisa get dressed while I pulled the car up front. She was wheeled down in a wheel chair just as she came in. I took her Mama home and JaLisa and I dropped the prescriptions off at the drive thru pharmacy. I told the girl behind the glass that I would be back to pick them up.

~ JALISA ~

I opened my eyes and I'm lying in my bed. It's 2am and I swear I'm hallucinating. My body feels numb and my mouth tastes like chalk. Richards lying beside me and he's snoring. I've never heard him snore before he must be real tired. I can't remember what day it is but I think its Christmas. When I try to stand I can't I'm seeing double so I sit back down on the bed. I'm sitting on the bed and rubbing my fingers through my hair. Okay I remember taking my braids out. I have to get up so I hold onto the side of the bed and walk out of the room. I'm holding onto the wall and I'm remembering passing out in the bathroom and Richard seeing the blood in the toilet. I shake my head because I don't want to remember what happened next. I just need something to drink my throat is so dry. I make it to the kitchen and open the fridge the light hurts my eyes so I grab the grapefruit juice and look at how much Vodka is missing from my bottle and I remember.

"Oh shit it worked."

When I turn on the light on top of the stove it all comes back to me. On the night of Christmas Eve after Richard falls asleep I came to the kitchen and poured myself a glass of Vodka and mixed it with Castor Oil and drank it fast. I went to lay back down with Richard and fell asleep. When I woke up it must have worked I look down under Richard's T-shirt that I'm wearing and I have on these huge drawers and a pad. I don't ever wear pads. On the dinning room table is all the medicine they must have given me in the hospital. I grab the papers off the table and the doctor's notes say that I had a miscarriage at 16 weeks of pregnancy. Cause unknown.

"Thank you Lord for answering my prayers I pray that my baby is with you in heaven because I know that I was not ready to have that baby."

There are more pads here on the table so I go to the bathroom and change and get back into the bed with Richard. Damn I didn't get a chance to give Richard his presents yesterday I get back out the bed and turn on the night light to get his stuff I brought from Sawgrass Mills Mall with Jasmine.

"Damn Jasmine is going to be so sad."

When I reach for Richard's gifts I smile when I knock over the box that held all the jewelry that Terrible T. gave me. I miss Terrible T. I have to call him as soon as I get a moment away from Richard.

"Baby, what are you doing in the closet?"

I grab the jewelry and stuff it in the box and hid it under some of my shoes.

"I was looking for your Christmas gift baby that's all."

I walked out the closet with his packages and he smiled. His eyes are all puffy like he's been crying. He stood up half sleep and hugged me. I turned the ceiling light on even though it burned both our eyes and we kissed.

He asked, "Are you okay baby?"

"Yes I am. I'm sad but I'm okay with what happened."

"Baby you are so strong."

"Only when I'm with you."

He looked at the engraved money clip and started laughing.

He said, "I always wanted one of these."

"I'm glad you like it."

"Its 3 o'clock in the morning let's go back to bed."

"Okay baby."

We held each other until the sun came up.

~ RICHARD ~

The sun came in through the blinds and I swear I ain't had no sleep. JaLisa is up so early and it's Sunday. I thought I was gonna sleep in.

"Let's go rent the truck today."

"Huh?"

"Yeah I want you to move your stuff in today."

"Okay but . . ."

"But . . . What? We can do it by ourselves."

"You can't lift nothin."

"I know but you can."

"What about a day of rest."

"Come on baby do this for me."

"Now how can I say no to that face?"

"You can't so get up and let's get moving."

We left the house at 9 o'clock and it took us an hour to find a van. I don't have a whole lot of shit that I'm moving so we didn't need a huge truck. The crazy thing is I have to move all this shit by myself cause JaLisa can't lift a thing even though she keeps trying. It's like she is intentionally trying to hurt herself. I leave in a week from today to go back to New York and I have to know that she's gonna be okay before I just up and leave.

There's a lot of stuff that I threw in the trash that I'm just not taking to JaLisa's. The main things are my clothes, shoes, TV's and pictures of my parents. All of my household stuff I packed up for the Good Will. I will drop that stuff off on my way back to JaLisa's. She packed up my CD's and DVD and was excited to see so many old albums that my parents left me.

I even have an old record player that was in the back of one of my closets and we are bringing that with us too.

JaLisa's cell rings and it must be Jasmine I heard her say girl shut up about three times before she walked outside and sat in the van. When we finally empty the apartment I dropped the keys in an envelope and give them to the rental office. There's no fees that I owe cause I'm on a month to month lease. When I got to the van she told Jasmine that she had to go and she hung up the phone.

~ JaLisa ~

When my cell rings its Jasmine's cell number on the caller ID, so I answer.

"What's up girl?"

"What do you mean what's up? I borrowed my Mama's car so I could come see your ass and I get here and you ain't here."

"I know girl sorry I'm helping Richard move."

"Move what? Bitch didn't you just lose the baby yesterday and you helping that nigga move?"

"Jasmine shut up! I'm not lifting anything I'm just sitting here watching."

"He could be doing that and you could be in the bed."

"In the bed for what? I'm okay."

"But JaLisa you don't have any emotions ova losing the baby do you?"

"Yeah but I can't let it get the best of me I have to move on."

"Move on JaLisa it was just yesterday and on Christmas."

"I know girl a day I'll never forget as long as I live."

"When am I going to get to see you? We need to talk."

"Okay well I don't know . . . Hey Richard's walking towards the van I gotta go."

Richard opens the driver door to the van and say, "You didn't have to get off the phone."

"No that was just Jasmine fussing about me not being home when she came ova. She said I should be in the bed."

"Well at least we do think alike cause that's exactly where you are going as soon as we drop this stuff at Good Will and take the truck back."

"When we take your stuff back to my house I'm not gonna go with you to take the truck back. I'll just take my medicine and lay down for a while."

"Now you're talkin' some sense."

He leaned over and we kissed Richard leaves in a week and will be gone for a month. I have to get my shit together so by the time he gets back things will be in order. I plan to go to work tomorrow to talk to Brenda and I know I'm pushing it but it's just some things I need to get done and over with. I was thinking about buying a new car but since Richard's gonna leave his car here with me I still have time. I have so many plans with the money he's giving me. He said he's going to the bank in the morning to do the transfer and I'll have him take me to work on his way.

When Richard finally unloaded the van we moved all of his things into the extra room and I promised him that I would go through everything and put it where it should go. As soon as I saw him pull off in the van I called Terrible T. and he answered.

He said, "Hello."

"Hi Terrible T. it's me JaLisa."

"Hey baby girl how are you? Merry Christmas I thought you would have called me before now."

"I wanted to Terrible T. but Richard has been here."

"Oh okay. You miss me?"

"Hell yeah I miss you when you coming to see me?"

"As soon as he gets on the plane next week and I'll come down there."

"Okay that sounds real good."

"How you been feelin?"

"Not so good. Terrible T. I lost the baby yesterday."

"Damn JaLisa I'm sorry to hear that. How you holdin up?"

"I'll be okay. I just need a hug."

"Well I've got all that and then some."

I hope he don't hear me smiling through the phone.

"I'm looking forward to it Terrible T."

"I'm gon spoil you girl just wait. Imma have a whole day planned when I get down there. You gon love it."

"Okay Terrible T. I gotta go now. I'll call you next week."

"A'aight."

I told Richard last night that I was going to work so when my alarm clock went off this morning he wasn't real surprised. He did ask why I needed to go in today but I just told him that I needed to do this.

When I walked in the office my co-workers asked was everything okay and was there anything they could do for me and I just smiled and thanked them. Brenda was not in her office she had an 8 0'clock meeting and would be in around 10AM was what I was told by one of my co-workers. I immediately sat at my desk and started typing my resignation letter via email.

To: Hicks, Brenda
CC: Botch, Elizabeth
From: Wright, JaLisa

Subject: Letter of Resignation

This letter is to advise you effective immediately I will no longer be able to provide my services at TLC Incorporated. I apologize for any inconvenience this may cause you or your staff and I thank you for all of your support in the past two years that I have been employed here.

Sincerely,
JaLisa Wright

I printed a copy for my personal files and pressed SEND on my email. It feels so good to finally be done and over with this place. I walked to the back of the office to the storage room and found two banker boxes to pack my things in. When I got back to my desk one of my co-workers asked where was I going and I told her that this was my last day.

She said, "Just like that?"

I said, "Just like that!"

I took my time and deleted all of the personal emails that I did not need. The ones I needed I forwarded those to my Yahoo account. The next thing on my list to do was to plug up the shredder and get rid of anything I did want to leave behind. I had so much stuff to shred that I had to dump the bag three times. I took down the picture that I had of Mama and Daddy that I had taped to the wall. I stuck that in an inner office envelope and laid it in the box. I have about a hundred post-it notes in all different colors so I trash the one's pertaining to work. The personal ones I stick to a blank piece of copy paper and lay in it in the box. I have two of my school books here and those I stack neatly in my box. When I unplugged my clock radio it read 9:30AM. I have thirty more minutes to wrap things up. I can't believe all of this stuff that I have collected over the past two years. I even saved the dead roses that Richard sent me last Valentine's Day. After I threw all the junk I wound up needing only one box. I called Richard on his cell and he answered.

"What's up baby?"

"I'll be ready at 10:15."

"Cool cause I'm finished at the bank. I'll be waiting in the parking lot."

"See you then."

As I was walking back from washing out my vase Brenda walked in and my heart sank.

She said, "Glad to see you could join us."

I smiled and said, "Please check our email and let me know if you'd like to see me."

She hurried to her desk and was calling me over the intercom.

"Yes Brenda."

"Please come into my office."

I took my time since it was nothing she could do to change my mind about leaving today. I put tape on the top of my box and sat it on top of my desk. When I got in Brenda's office I had the silliest smirk on my face.

"You wanted to see me before I leave?"

"What brought about this so sudden?"

"Well, where should I start?"

"You can start with why?"

"Because Brenda you are obnoxious as hell. I am sick of coming in here every day of the week making you look good and you making me look like shit to Mrs. Botch."

"JaLisa I do not make you look like shit."

"Look, are you going to let me talk or what?"

"Okay talk then JaLisa."

"Remember my thugged out boyfriend?"

"Yes, his name is Richard right."

"I'm glad you remembered his name. Well anyway he received a recording contract for over one million dollars and he told me that I don't ever have to work again."

After saying that I held out my huge diamond ring across her desk and said, "He proposed to me."

Brenda's mouth dropped open and she was speechless for the first time in the two years that she has been my boss. I am so happy to finally be done with her and this stale ass office. I got up and said to her, "Thank you for everything you have honestly taught me a lot."

Brenda just looked at me still with nothing to say so I left her office grabbed my box and headed for the door. I was real low profile because I didn't want to answer any questions. Instead of taking the elevator I took the back stairs and walked around to the parking lot where Richard was parked. Just like that my employment with TLC Incorporated was over and I feel like a ton of bricks have been lifted off my shoulders.

Richard got out of the car and took the box from me and put in the truck. He kissed me on the lips and handed me my bank slip. I hugged Richard so tight and fell into his arms. After everything I have been through over the last few days this is one of the happiest moments in my life. I finally have financial freedom.

When we got home I wanted to make love to Richard but he reminded me that the doctor told him that I needed six weeks to recover from the trauma that my body went through after losing the baby.

~ RICHARD ~

The week wasn't even ova and I got a call from Terrible T.'s assistant. I looked at my cell as it rang before I picked it up.

"Hello."

"Hi Richard, how are you?"

"I'm cool."

"Look I was talking to your publicist this morning and she wants you to come back to New York ASAP. Do you think that will be possible?"

"What's up why do I need to come back so soon?"

"There's some publicity stuff that we need you to do on Friday morning on three different radio stations. So that means you will have interviews at 7am, 9am and 11am. All in different parts of the city."

"That sounds great but I have to talk to my fiancée first to see how she feels about it. She's been through a lot this week and I want to make sure she's okay I'll call you back in about an hour."

"Okay but make sure you do because I will make all your travel arrangements."

When I got off the phone I went to the room to break the news to JaLisa.

"Hey baby we need to talk."

"What's up Richard?"

"Terrible T.'s assistant called to say that I need to be in town for radio interviews on Friday morning. So I have to leave by Thursday night."

"That's cool baby I'll come see you in a couple of weeks."

"You promise?"

"Yes baby I promise as soon as I get my school situation straight I will be there. I'll stay with you for a few days okay."

"That's a bet let me call her back so she can make the arrangements."

~ JaLisa ~

s soon as Richard's plane took off my cell phone rang. It's Terrible
T., "Hello Terrible T. Richard just took off."
"I know, I had my assistant make all the arrangements."
"What?"
"Yeah I told her to call him to do the radio publicity and I had her
make all of his arrangements."
"So where are you know Terrible T.?"
"I'm in a private condo on North Miami Beach. The address is 7901
Collins Avenue, Suite 1152."
"Terrible T. I wasn't expecting you I need to go home and change."
"Okay but its 4 o'clock now and I what I have planned for you will
begin at 5:30pm."
When I hung up from Terrible T. I was a ball of nerves. I can't believe
he set all this up. I'm gonna go and see him and enjoy him while he's here
but I have to end this. I can't go on doing this to Richard if he ever found
out he would no doubt kill me.
I drove about 100mph to get home and changed. My hair looks totally
different than it did the last time he saw me. So I pinned it up and stuck
a couple of hair pins in. I run my wash cloth under the water in the sink
and wipe myself off. I ran to my closet and pulled one of the outfits that
he brought me out the back with along the Monolo heels. I couldn't wear
all the jewelry because it would have over done the outfit so I only put on
the earrings and bracelet.
Once I finished I ran to the car and headed for North Beach. I know
exactly where he is there's a hotel right next to the condo with a 70's theme

that I like to go to. It was called the Dezerland but I think they changed the name.

So I got my breathing together and ride the elevator up to the 11th floor. When I ring the bell Terrible T. comes to the door and he's on his cell phone. Damn he looks good enough to eat right about now. He's talking to his assistant and she's confirming that Richard made it there and the driver has already picked him up to take him to his hotel.

He turns the phone off and placed it on his side and grabs me in his arms. "I missed you Terrible T."

"I missed you too JaLisa that's why I'm all the way down here."

"So what do you have planned?"

"There's a driver down stairs ready to take us to Fort Lauderdale. Are you ready?"

"Yes, but where . . . ?"

Before I could get my words out he leaned down and kissed my lips and licked my neck. Damn I am getting so moist right now and I just want to rip his clothes off. I moved my hand to his pants and felt him become hard. I have not had sex since before I lost the baby and my body is aching right now. Terrible T. backed up and said, "We'll have enough time for that later."

"Terrible T. but I want you right now."

"Come on this is supposed to be a surprise to make you feel better."

"Shit I feel better right now."

We walked out to the elevator and an old couple got on with us. They didn't recognize Terrible T. and that's a good thing. I positioned my body in front of him and the old lady eyebrows raised, I know she was calling me every freak in the book.

It took us about twenty minutes to get out to Fort Lauderdale and when we got there the driver pulled into a dock where these huge Yachts where. Terrible T. pointed to the one that we would be riding on and I had to blink twice. This big ass shit has to be over a million dollars and we are just strolling on board like he owns the thing.

Terrible T. said, "This is the same Yacht I used in one of my videos and whenever I come to town I always get the hookup."

"Terrible T. this is so amazing."

"You are so amazing JaLisa."

When we got inside this house on water everything was set in cherry wood. The cushions were pure white and made of soft leather. He took me in one of the cabins as we set sail and we began to play. Terrible T. lifted my top over my head and grabbed both my breasts in his hands. He is definitely a breast man he always goes for my breasts first. My bra unhooked in the front so it was real easy for him to remove. I could feel us moving in the water and kinda glad that we came back here in the room because I've never been out in the water like this before. I have no idea where he is taking me to but I am along for the ride. My p---- is throbbing right now and all I can think of is Richard saying that I am supposed to wait six weeks but to hell with that. Terrible T. sits down on bed and pulls me on top of him he's going from one breast to the other and he's so hard I can feel him poking my leg. I unbutton his shirt and remove it. Instead of throwing it on the floor I lay it across one of the chairs next to the bed. Terrible T. begins to suck on my neck and usually I would be uncomfortable with this but I know that I'm not gonna see Richard for a couple of weeks so I don't mind. I took of the wife-beater that Terrible T. was wearing and tossed it across the chair. He stood me up and slid down my pants as I took off my heels. I'm standing here with only a thong on and Terrible T. spins me around.

He says, "You have a beautiful body JaLisa have you ever thought about being in music videos?"

"No Terrible T. I haven't I never looked at myself like that."

"Well you should. What would say if I wanted to put you in my next video?"

"I would say that Richard would have a fit."

Terrible T. pulled down my thong and started licking on me as I stood right in front of him. My body feels so good. Terrible T. seems to be so fascinated by my piercing. He stuck his tongue all the way inside me and I felt my body begin to cum. This shit feels so good. He lay back on the bed and told me to sit on his face and of course I did. I rode his face until my legs got weak. I lifted my body off Terrible T. and unbuttoned his pants and let them fall to the floor. We are all ova each other and put him in my mouth and he said, "Damn JaLisa your mouth is so warm."

With a full mouth I said, "You like that Terrible T.?"

"Hell yeah, damn your mouth is so wet and warm it feels like a p----."

I almost choked when I burst out laughing. I never heard that before.

Terrible T. started moving his body while he was in my mouth and suddenly his body froze. I slid my tongue along the head of him and then ran my tongue up the side. I could see his toes curl in his socks he is really loving this right now.

"Shit JaLisa you gon make me cum in your mouth!"

"Please do I love the way you taste."

"Oh shit!"

Terrible T. came and I drank every ounce of him. His body was so tense afterward but he still wanted some more so I gave it to him. He reached down to his pants to get his wallet but was very weak so I got it for him. I took his wallet out and in there is a picture of Miz Thang' I started to get bothered by this but why should I'm here with him and she's off making videos some where. I pulled out one of the condoms and slid it on him. Once I did that I sat on top of him I sat on top and rode him until my insides started to ache.

"Oh Terrible T.!"

My eyes rolled back into my head as Terrible T. pulled me down on him. My entire body feels numb.

"Oh shit Terrible T."

When I look down it feels like I am bleeding but I'm not, my body Is cumming. I love the way he makes me feel. Terrible T. turns me over and started hitting it from the back. My insides are throbbing and I am cumming again Terrible T feels me cumming and he does as well and falls on top of me. Our bodies are exhausted. And sex is in the air. There is a little bathroom big enough for both of us to squeeze into so step into the glass shower. This is so cute it looks like we are in a little dollhouse.

Terrible T. turns me around in the shower and washed my back and I do the same to him. I feel so close to him right now but I know that I need to end this because it just ain't right. Terrible T. leaned me against the wall and got on one knee and started sucking on me again. He really knows what he's doing and has no problem pleasing me.

"Damn Terrible T. this is great."

He allows me to cum in his mouth before we get out and dry off. After we dress he holds my hand and leads me out to the deck.

"Wow!" Is all I can say, the view is spectacular. We are totally surrounded by water and the sun is beginning to set on the ocean. I have never seen a sun set this way and I tell Terrible T.

"I have never been out in the water like this before. I've gone on paddle boats and jet skis but nothing ever like this."

"JaLisa I want to take you around the world to do things so that you can always say. Damn Terrible T. I've never done this before."

"But Terrible T . . ."

"But what JaLisa I know you think this is wrong but this feels so right. Shit I have a girl too but why deny myself from what feels right?"

"That's deep Terrible T."

We watch as the sun looks like its being swallowed up by the ocean. The sky is a beautiful color of orange and I am just melting in Terrible T.'s arms.

There's this young spanish guy on the boat with us that brings us a bottle of Cristal in a gold bucket of ice. I asked Terrible T., "Do you have Cristal waiting where ever you go."

"All around the world it's my favorite."

The sun continued to go down and the yachts lights came on. The entire atmosphere was extremely intimate. I have to experience this type of stuff with Richard but I wonder would he be open to it.

Terrible T. said, "Look JaLisa I know you don't think this is right but I ain't about to let you go just like that."

"What do you mean Terrible T.?"

"I'm not playing no games with you. I know that you want to back away from this especially since Richard has his deal and you want to make things work but it's not that simple."

"But . . . Terrible T."

"No listen to me. I'm being serious it's not over until I say it's over."

I've never seen him look at me this way. I didn't even know he had that side to him.

"Terrible T. you're scaring me."

"I don't want you to be scared I just want you know that it's not ova till I say so."

Terrible T. grabbed my face and started kissing me for some strange reason this shit is turning me on. What does he mean till he says its ova. Terrible T. pulled down my pants slid on another condom and forced me on top of him.

"Damn Terrible T."

"Did you hear what I said JaLisa?"

"Yes Terrible T. I heard you."

He slammed me on top of him and it hurts but it's a good hurt. I love the way he is handling me. I'm facing him and looking out into ocean and the sun is finally set. Jasmine pops in my mind and I have to remember to call her. She is not going to believe this and I hope she's still not trippin off me not being home the other day. Terrible T. has me riding him and my p---- is throbbing. I really do believe he is trying to make a point but it's over when I say its ova not him.

"JaLisa if you leave me I will cancel Richard's contract."

"Terrible T. you can't do that."

"It's my company and I can do what eva I want."

"But that's not fair."

"What wouldn't be fair is if you tried to stop seeing me."

He's making me cum, "Oh Terrible T. what are you doing to me. Damn you feel so good inside me."

"And I want to always make you feel this way."

"I'm not gonna break it off. Oh shit! I promise."

As I said, that Terrible T. came so hard that it started to leak out the condom. I jumped up and took the towel from the bucket and wiped him off.

He said, "See that's what I like about you. You are so considerate. And every time we are together you really take care of me."

"That's because I care about you Terrible T."

"I know that's exactly what I mean you care about Terrible T. Not my money or my status nor do you care about my career and that is very rare."

"Terrible T. I know every one you meet is not just about your celebrity status."

"Shit I can't tell."

"Damn Terrible T. that has to be tough."

"Yeah it is because you don't know who to trust."

"So you're saying that you trust me?"

"I wouldn't be here if I didn't JaLisa."

"That means a lot Terrible T."

We sailed until midnight as we just drifted along the ocean. Terrible T. and I went into the cabin and held each other until the sun came peaking in. My body is so relaxed that I don't want to move. The man that gave us the Cristal last night served us breakfast in bed and that is where we stayed until it was time to dock.

Terrible T. said, "I have to get back to New York to take care of some business. Do you wanna come?"

"No, but I will be there in a couple of weeks. We can meet then."

"That sounds good but aren't you coming up there to be with Richard."

"Yes but I can make some time for you Terrible T."

The driver was waiting for us when we got off the Yacht and drove us back to the condo. I followed Terrible T onto the elevator where we kissed and he said, "Damn JaLisa I'm gonna miss you."

"I'm gonna miss you too Terrible T but I'll be up there soon enough."

He's not being as forceful as he was last night but he backed me into the wall and we kissed he ran his tongue down my neck and turned me to face the wall. He put his last condom on and bent me over still facing the wall and took it from behind. My body just quivered as he continued to penetrate me.

"Damn Terrible T. you gonna miss this p----, huh?"

"Hell yeah Imma miss this p----."

Terrible T. just kept pounding me until he felt himself getting ready to cum and he picked me up and carried me into the bedroom.

"Terrible T. what are you doing?"

"I'm making love to you."

"What did you say? You're doing what?"

"I . . . I'm making love to you."

"Terrible T. how could you say that? You don't love me!"

"Shit JaLisa I love what you do for me and how you make me feel. Why I can't say what I feel?"

Our bodies released simultaneously.

I know he had to get back to New York but I wanted him to stay another night. I could lay here and make love to him if that's what he wants to call it all night if I had the chance.

He got a call on his cell. It was his assistant confirming that his flight was scheduled to leave in an hour and strongly suggested that he make it to the airport.

"Damn baby I gotta go."

"I know I promise I will come see you soon."

He kissed me so passionately before I left that it really did feel like he was beginning to fall for me but not someone like him. Not Terrible T., he has such an ego how could he fall for someone like me?

When I left my head was in the clouds. I got back home to see that Richard had left messages on the house phone and my cell.

When I called him back he didn't pick up so I left him a message just to let him know that I was okay and I needed some time to think about every thing. This is really big and I don't know what to do about it.

I called Jasmine and she said she was going to borrow her mother's car. When I hung up the phone I ran my bath water and unlocked the door so she could let herself in. My p---- is aching so bad that it needs a rest. I lay back in the water and must have dozed off because when I woke up Jasmine was standing over me and the water was cold.

"Hey girl you scared the shit out of me."

"Well you left the door open any one could have walked in."

"I knew you were on your way but I didn't know I was gonna fall asleep. How long have you been here?"

"About fifteen minutes."

"Oh."

Jasmine sat in Indian style on the floor next to the tub as I let out some of the cold water and ran all hot water. She just looked at me and said, "You look so beautiful without those braids."

"Thanks Jasmine that's so sweet."

It's the way she's looking at me that has me pulsating. I have been with Terrible T. all night and even this morning and it's something about the way that Jasmine is looking at me that is turning me on. I licked my lips and she leaned in towards me.

She asked, "Can I kiss you JaLisa."

Here I am wanting her to come over so I could talk to her about Terrible T. and she is making me hot.

"Yes, Jasmine you don't ever have to ask that unless we are not alone."

Just the taste of her lips had me wanting more. She sucked on my bottom lip the way Richard does and I am starting to throb again. What is going on? Why the hell am I so horny?

Jasmine slid back her sleeve and placed her hand in the water and gently rubbed my clit. It is so sore and she is really making it feel a lot better.

Jasmine said, "I love you JaLisa."

My eyes were about to pop out of my head and I said, "I love you too Jasmine."

I got up out of the water soaking wet and grabbed my towel and she followed me into my room. I laid back on the bed wet and all and Jasmine slid her tongue up and down my clit until my body started to tremble. She looked up at me and winked her eye.

"Oh Jasmine!" I can not believe I am sitting here calling out Jasmine's name. This shit is unreal. It's like she is massaging my clit with her tongue. It was so sore until she came over. Jasmine slid one of her fingers inside of me and I felt my body starting to come. She has one finger in me as she licks my clit. I love this.

"Oh my God Jasmine you have me cumming."

Jasmine laid her head on top of my stomach and I could hear her crying.

"What's wrong Jasmine?"

"JaLisa I really love you and I hate to see what you are going through."

"What do you mean?"

"I mean the way you made yourself lose the baby."

"What are you talking about . . . I didn't . . ."

"JaLisa don't lie to me I know you did something to that baby."

I am not about to sit here and tell her what I did to my baby she would never understand.

"Look Jasmine I will be okay but I was not ready to have that baby you and I both know that."

Jasmine got up and went to the bathroom and rinsed her mouth out she came back and I was still lying in my same position. She put her nose next to mine and licked her tongue over my lips and we started kissing again. She has me throbbing again but I swear my body can't cum any more I don't have anything left inside me so I rolled her over and slid down her pants and thong and let my tongue do the rest of the talking. I can't have her questioning me about this right now. Jasmine is squirming all ova the bed. I didn't know that I knew how to eat p---- but I guess I do because she seems to be enjoying herself. Jasmine grabbed my head and made me stay on this one spot instead of licking I sucked and she went wild.

"JaLisa what the hell are you doing down there?"

I took one of my fingers the same way she did me and stuck it inside her and sucked her clit at the same time.

"Oh shit JaLisa, damn girl where you learn that shit from?"

I didn't respond I just continued to suck. She came in no time and released herself all over my bed but it's all good I'll wash my comforter when she leaves.

"You like that Jasmine?"

"Like it bitch where did you learn to eat p---- like that?"

"I don't know I guess by having mine ate so much."

"That was great JaLisa I feel so relaxed."

The next thing I knew she laid on my bed and fell asleep. Shit I must me good I have her falling to sleep and shit. I pulled the covers over Jasmine and left the room. I go straight to the kitchen to pour myself and drink and it's not enough Vodka to even get me tipsy so I don't bother. I open the grapefruit juice and drink straight from the glass bottle.

I went into the living room with the juice in my hand and flopped down on the sofa and flipped the remote. The only thing on is videos and True Hollywood Stories so I flip back and forth between the two. As I'm watching the videos I lay back and close my eyes and I swear I'm dreaming when I hear Richards song come on. I open my eyes and his first video is playing on BET this is cool as shit. He in the studio and then clips of New York City flash across the screen. I grab the cordless and call him on his cell.

He answers on the first ring, "Hey baby where have you been?"

"I was home I was just getting some rest I took those pain pills last night after you left."

"I was getting worried about you."

"I'm okay I was watching BET and your video came on."

"Already I thought it would take a few more weeks."

"No I'm watching it right now. I love it especially you in the studio."

"Thanks baby it was all my idea."

"You are very creative."

"You think so?"

"Hell yeah this is so cool."

"Look I was approached by Terrible T.'s assistant after I did the radio shows this morning and she asked if I knew anyone that wanted to be in Terrible T.'s next video and the only one I thought of was you and Jasmine. Do ya'll want to come to New York in a few days?"

"Hell yeah Jasmine is going to be so excited."

"How about you are you exited?"

"I will be excited just seeing you baby."

I will call to have all the arrangements made and call you back with the details.

"Richard I am so proud of you."

"Thanks baby do you mean that."

"Of course I mean it I love how you are growing so fast."

When I got off the phone I ran and jumped on the bed and woke Jasmine up.

"Girl Terrible T. wants us to come to New York and be in his new video."

"What about Richard?"

"He's the one that asked me."

"What?"

"Yeah Terrible T. asked me yesterday but some how he had his assistant to mention it to Richard."

"That's crazy JaLisa but how can I say no to that?"

"Good so Richard is going to call us with the arrangements."

"Back to New York we go. will we be staying in the same room together?" Jasmine said with a smile.

"No I will be in Richard's room and you will have your own room and I will come to your room when you want me to."

Jasmine leaned over and started kissing me I am moist all ova again. She really does something to me. Only if she had a d--- I would be riding her right now.

I had to tell her, "Girl if you had a d--- I would be riding you right now."

She went to her purse and pulled out a strap on.

"I thought you would never ask I was afraid to show you earlier but since you brought it up."

"Where the hell did you get that from."

"I got it from the freak store on 22nd Avenue."

"How long have you had it?"

"For about six months."

"Who have you used it on?"

"This one girl that I've known for a long time."

"When were you going to tell me about this girl?"

"Are you gonna let me use it on you or are you gonna ask twenty-one questions?"

"Is it clean?"

"Yes it's clean JaLisa."

Jasmine bent me ova and made me get on my knees and pulled off my panties and started licking me from behind the next thing I know she's sliding this big ass plastic d--- inside my p---- and it actually feels good. It feels damn good and she got some rhythm going on too. I am getting so we I don't believe this Jasmine if hitting it from the back and she's doing a damn good job.

"Don't stop Jasmine."

I don't believe I am enjoying this so much. I am not a lesbian but I am having sex with a woman. What's up with that would I call myself bisexual or what?

"Tell me you love me JaLisa."

"Oh Jasmine, I love you!"

"Say it again!"

"I love Jasmine got damn girl you are tearing my p---- up."

"Oh shit JaLisa I am cumming. Oh shit girl I love the f--- out of you!"

"Me too Jasmine . . . Me too."

She laid her head on my back and started kissing it but we were not finished yet. She f---ed me and I just have to f--- her. There is so much cum on this damn plastic d--- I have to go in the bathroom and wipe it off. I didn't dry it I just put it on and began to ride Jasmine. She's looking into my eyes and telling me that she loves me and I believe her. She is so open right now and it's written all over her face. I am riding her like I ride Terrible T. and I feel in control. She has tears running down the side of her face so I lean over and kiss her eyes and ask her, "Jasmine why are you crying?"

"Because I have waited so long for this but I know that you don't feel the way about me that I feel about you."

"How you know that."

"I can just tell JaLisa."

We both came and I got up and went into the bathroom to take a shower. My body is covered in sweat and Jasmine has taken a lot out of me. When I step in she gets in behind me and I look at her real strange.

"Please let me do this with you JaLisa I have always wanted to do this."

"It's okay Jasmine I don't mind."

"Are you sure?"

"I'm sure."

The shower was nice and intimate. Instead of keeping the light on I lit two candles and jumped back in the shower. We washed each other slowly and seductively Jasmine started with my back and neck up around my ears. She washed down my arms and wrapped her arms around my breasts.

She's turning me on all ova again. She took the sponge and rubbed it across my belly and down in between my legs and I could feel my body releasing fluids. This girl has experience that she doesn't want to tell me about. She gets down on her knees and has her face to my ass and run the sponge over it as she works her way down between my thighs. She turned me around and washed between my legs as I allowed the shower to run down my back. Jasmine is so much more sensual than Richard and Terrible T. I pulled her up and washed her same as she washed me and just our bodies touching made my insides begin to pulsate. We are all soaped up and begin to kiss. I don't believe we are in here my hair is soaking wet and so is hers and water is splashing all over the floor and everything. Once the water washed us clean Jasmine gets back on her knees and goes to action on my clit. I almost tore down the shower curtain when I started to cum.

When we were wrinkled as prunes I suggest that we get out and go to the bed. My cordless phone is ringing and damn I don't want to answer it but I do any way. Jasmine is pissed and it's written all over her face.

"Hello." I say in a seductive tone.

"What are you over there doing?"

"Um . . . Nothing." Jasmine is on her knees and rolling her tongue against my clit ring.

"Then why do you sound like that?" Richard persisted.

"I just got out the shower and you know what I do in there when I'm alone."

"Well you won't be alone too much longer. I have a flight booked for you and Jasmine in two days."

"Wow that's soon."

"Yeah Terrible T. starts shooting his video tomorrow but the shot that you and Jasmine are going to be in will be in two more days. So you will fly in here in the morning and go straight to the location."

When I got off the phone with Richard I asked Jasmine, "Why you look like that when I answered the phone?"

"I don't know I couldn't help it."

"Well I'm telling you this now. We leave for New York in two days and you are not going to be able to act like this when we get there."

"Okay but . . ."

"Look Jasmine let's talk."

Jasmine didn't want to talk she wanted to kiss, touch and rub and I was trying to be serious.

"We have to start packing Jasmine."

"We will just let me take care of you first I know you want some more."

She wasn't lying about that because I did want more and that is exactly what she gave me. I was so exhausted by the time we finished that I had to take a nap. When I woke up Jasmine was gone and she left a note on the table.

Hey Girl,

I'm out I will see you when it's time to get on the plane. I need some time to cool off. You've got my head spinning so bad I feel dizzy.

Love U,

P. S.
Call me later if you still want to talk . . .

I took the note crumbled it up and threw it in the trash. Then I went to my closet and pulled out my suitcase so that I could begin to pack.

When Jasmine and I got off the plane at LaGuardia Airport there was a driver to take us to the hotel to drop our things off. The front desk attendant was instructed by Richard to give me his keycard and Jasmine had a room right down the hall. We didn't even have a chance to settle in before my cell phone was ringing.

"Hey baby, have you made it to the hotel yet?"

"Yes I'm in your room now."

"Okay grab Jasmine and go back out to the car, he was instructed to take you to the video location."

"That's cool baby but where are you."

"I'm in the studio I won't be able to get over there before it's time for ya'll to finish up so I will meet you at the room tonight."

"Okay baby that's a bet."

When I hung up with Richard I walked down to Jasmine's room. She has been acting real funny since we got on the plane but I didn't say anything to her about it. When I knocked on the door she snatches it open.

"What's up?"

"Richard just called he said the driver was instructed to take us to video site right now."

She just brushed me off and said, "Okay let me grab my purse."

We rode the elevator down without a word and got into the back of the car. The driver rode down the separating glass window and asked did we want to stop for anything. We said no at the same time.

"What's up Jasmine? Why are you acting so shady?"

"Look JaLisa I'm trying to protect my feelings and preserve our friendship so I need to back off you that's all."

"Oh . . . well excuse me."

"Girl I'm not trying to be funny it's just that you've got Richard, Terrible T. and me and who do I have JaLisa?"

"I never looked at it like that Jasmine."

I leaned in and put my head on her shoulder and she rubbed her fingers through my hair. I really never thought about it like that I just pretty much always thought about myself and how I was feeling but she does have a point. When we got to the video location we just blended in with all that was going on. Terrible T. and I made eye contact and he gave me a wink.

Jasmine was in one scene and I was in another so we had to split up for the entire day. Terrible T. and I were alone for one moment and he whispers to me "You are looking so hot."

"Thank you Terrible T. and you are too."

He said, "Look I've been thinking about the other night and how I said it ain't ova until I say so well that ain't right."

"I know how you were feeling and I've been doing a lot of thinking and I realize that I need to be faithful to Richard. I need to at least try to make things work between us."

"I understand that JaLisa and after this video if you don't ever want to talk to me that's fine."

"No I wouldn't do you like that Terrible T. but as far as us be intimate we need to chill."

He gave me a hug as though it was the last time I was ever going to see him and we continued with the remainder of the video. Once the video was over the driver took Jasmine and I back to the hotel. Before Richard could get there Jasmine and I sat down in the restaurant and had dinner and just talked we decided that it was best not to be intimate again so that I could work things out with Richard. She leaned over the table and kissed me on my lips and we had a good laugh about all that has been going on. We promised to not let what we shared change our friendship but I'm sure it will. So I have learned I can't just only think about myself but I have to take into consideration the feelings of others.

~ RICHARD ~

Monica texted me at 11:11pm the message read "U R GONNA B A GRT DADDY." I powered the phone off and prayed that JaLisa could not read my expression. She decided to stay in New York with me for a few more days after she did the video for Terrible T. I'm jive mad that I didn't think about putting her in my first video but I really neva wanted to tie her into my music thang I felt that business and pleasure should be separate. She walks out of the little kitchen they have set up here in our hotel room and I see a look on her face. She is still wearing her hair and make up she had in the video and all I can think about is tappin that ass. I really don't even think she heard the phone go off and even if she did she may have thought it's was about the business anyway.

She was lookin so good I had to hit that . . .

She fell asleep before I did so I closed the room door behind me and grabbed my phone off the night stand. I went down stairs to the lobby and decided to chill at the bar for a minute. I dialed Monica back at the number she text me from and she answered after the third ring.

"What's up Boo?" she answers.

"Hey what's up shawty I got your text earlier what's that all about? I told you JaLisa lost my baby."

"No boo I was texting you to tell you that you about to be a daddy. I'm two months pregnant and I decided I'm gonna keep the baby."

"What? You bullshittin?"

"I know you wit JaLisa but I thought you would be happy."

"How . . . how this happen . . . ?" I questioned.

"Do you really need me to refresh your memory?"

"Nah but I'm sayin though."

"You sayin what?"

"I was strapped up most of the time."

"You right you was strapped most of the time I even brought some of the condoms myself."

"Damn Shawty how could this happen?"

"I wasn't too happy myself Richard I found out about a month ago and I kept tryin to call you but got no answer that's when I decided that I would do it on my own if I had to."

"Nah man I don't . . . I mean I don't know what to say."

"You don't have to say anything I'm not askin you for nothing I make decent money and I can take care of myself."

"But Monica I don't mean it like that . . . I'm just sayin. I don't know what I'm sayin."

"So you alright with this?"

"It seems I don't have a choice in the decision I can't tell you what to do with your body I can't tell you not to have the baby. It's just messed up right now with my girl losing my son and all and with this type of news I just may lose her too."

"I don't want to break up you and your girl Richard I just wanted to let you know what I have been dealing with since I got back to Atlanta."

"I'm coming back down south in a couple of weeks and I will stop thru to see you so we can sit down and talk. How does that sound?"

"That sounds good."

"A'aight Shawty I gotta go. Give me a few days I'll call you and let you know exactly when I'm coming down."

I feel real messed up right now. Talking to Monica has got my head all messed up. I'm sitting in this cold as bar after midnight and I just want to break down . . .

~JALISA~

I decided to come back to the University of Miami for my junior year fall semester. Richard wanted me to stay in New York with him but I found that he was at the condo a lot less once he went on tour as an opening act for Terrible T. New York although it's exciting to be there I didn't have any friends outside of Richard's circle of industry friends and groupies so I got bored.

It's been almost a month since I've last seen Richard although I talk to him on the phone at least once a day. Terrible T. still calls and gives me the latest updates of the tour and still tries to get at me. He keeps asking to come see me once the tour is over but as I explained it to him when the tour is over Richard will be coming home for a while. T. acts as if he wants to tell me something each time I speak with him but whatever it is he always talks around it.

Jasmine and I hang out often she still flirts with me but has a girlfriend now. The two met a couple of years ago as Jasmine explains but they ran into each other at a club one night and have been inseparable ever since. Her name is Chanel and I met her once when I stopped by Jasmines' mother's house they were all there. Chanel seemed to be a little shy and distant so I asked Jasmine had she told her about what we shared and she swore she didn't but it didn't feel that way. Chanel kept avoiding eye contact with me and even got up and went to Jasmine's bedroom and stayed there until I left.

I'm sitting in Communications Class and these chairs are so uncomfortable my back and ankles are hurting and I am just ready to get up and call it a day. Since Richard pays all my bills and has given me spending money I don't have to work so I started going to the school's gym that was recently renovated. I have to do this to refocus some of this energy I have going on inside of me.

Since Richard has been in New York and Jasmine and I have been on a chill I have been extremely horny and no way to let out my frustrations besides going to the gym. My thoughts were interrupted by Professor Thomas. "I will need each of you to pair up into groups of two and this will be your partner for the remainder of the semester."

Oh God here we go with this again! I just sat in my same spot as everyone assembled themselves into groups. When I looked around the room everyone seemed to have a group formed except for this one girl in the back of the room. So instead of waiting for her to come over to me I picked up all of my stuff and went to where she's sitting. Her name is Ramona and she's originally from New York which caught my attention right away.

Professor Thomas spoke again "Ok class I want you to take about ten minutes to get to know one another and then I am going to allow you to take a break and when we come back there will be another task."

I asked Ramona to tell me about herself first. She said, "My name is Ramona Hernandez. My mother is black and my father is Cuban. I'm twenty-five years old. I don't have any children and I am here because I was accepted into the Nursing program on a full academic scholarship. I have a condo on the beach that is actually my parents and I'm staying there at least until I finish school. I've visited Miami every year since I was ten and I am considering staying here once I graduate. My only concern is the hurricanes since I do stay on the beach."

As she talked all I could do was watch her lips and the light pink shade of lip gloss she was wearing. I wondered who it was made by because it made lips shine so perfectly. My heart began to beat really fast and I seemed to have trouble breathing until she interrupted my thoughts.

"Okay JaLisa enough of my rambling now it's your turn."

I smiled and tried to gather my thoughts. "Okay yes . . . my name is JaLisa."

"I was born and raised in Miami. My major is Journalism and I am black, don't know if I'm mixed with anything but my mother says we are part Cherokee Indian. I don't have any children and I am engaged although we haven't set a date. I have townhouse in North Miami and although I have lived here all my life and I still get nervous about the hurricanes. My fiancé' has me traveling often between New York and Miami because he is in the music industry and is always on the go now."

Ramona's eyes lit up when I mentioned Richard was in the music industry.

She said, "I knew you looked very familiar you look exactly like this girl in Terrible T. new video."

"Yeah that was me." I said as I let out a long sigh.

"That is so cool did you meet him through your boyfriend, I mean fiancé?"

"Well actually that's a long story but I guess you can say that."

"So how often do you go up to New York?"

"I haven't been in about a month but I usually go every couple of weeks since Richard signed his contract."

"You mean to tell me that Richie is your fiancé! Oh my God . . . I don't know what to say. So why are you here and not on tour with him?"

"Because girl that's *his* thing."

"I would be traveling the country with my man."

"Yeah you say that now but when you see all the groupies and get left behind for days on end in a hotel room you get bored and start to think of other things to do besides shop."

Professor Thomas interrupted our conversations with "Okay now what I want each of you to do is to stand up and tell us a few things about the person that is in your group I would like to see how well you were listening to them."

She then went around the room and you could tell who was listening to the person in their group and who wasn't. She finally got to us and I repeated back everything that Ramona told me about herself and she did the same only she left out the part about Richard and Terrible T.

We looked at each other and winked when class was over we stayed behind for a few moment and talked. She asked, "So what are you doing tonight?"

"I don't have any plans, my girl Jasmine and I usually hang out but she's all booed up so I'm solo. How about you, what are you doing?"

"There's this poetry lounge that I go to on Tuesday nights it's small but everyone there is real cool and down to earth that usually starts about 9 o'clock you wanna come?"

"That sounds cool where is it?"

"The spot is on Fifth and Collins Avenue on South Beach do you have a morning class tomorrow?"

"No, why you ask?"

"Well the poetry readings usually last about an hour we can just hang out after that."

We exchanged cell phone numbers and I agreed to call her about 8 o'clock.

On my way home I kept thinking about her pink lip gloss and her lips for some reason. I got all warm again I had to laugh to myself. My cell rings it's Jasmine, "What's up girl?" I asked.

"Ain't shit just checkin you."

"I thought I wasn't gonna hear from you?"

"Why you say that?"

"Cause you been all booed up."

"JaLisa please I ain't hardly . . . well I guess."

"Yeah I know you have been!"

"Okay but it is what it is."

"I know Jasmine that's why I haven't been calling you. Chanel acted like she had a serious problem with me when I came over to your mom's house."

"Nah she cool she's just a little shy and she thinks that you have a problem with her."

"Well I don't you are my best friend and I feel left out since ya'll been seeing each other."

"Don't be like that JaLisa we can hang out what you doing tonight?"

"This girl Ramona invited me to this poetry lounge on South Beach."

"Poetry Lounge?"

"Is she talking about The Freeze on Fifth and Collins?"

"Well that's the street but she ain't say the name why what's wrong with that place."

"Girl the majority of the kids in there are either gay or bi."

"Jasmine I don't even care I just need to get out of the house ever since I've been back from New York I've been in the damn house."

"A'aight J. call me tomorrow and let me know how it was."

"Okay maybe we can hook up this weekend."

"Just let me know we can all go out me, you Chanel and your new friend."

"Jasmine, that sounds like a double date."

She hung up the phone without responding that girl be trippin every since we hooked up a few months ago she has been straight trippin. She's the one all booed up and gon try to hate on me when I say I need to get out the damn house. I'm so distracted by what she said about the Poetry Lounge that I sat through the damn green light by the time the cars started blowing behind me the light was turning red again.

When I walked in my front door I could see the answering machine light on. I dropped my keys and purse on the couch and pressed play. There were three messages the first was Mama.

"Hey baby . . . it's me Mama call me when you get in. I made an appointment to get my car serviced on Friday and I need you to follow me so I won't be sitting there waiting all day." Beep.

The next message is Richard.

"How's my girl? I miss you. I was gonna call your cell but I know you got class on Tuesday. Holla at me later we got a few more weeks of tour and I'll be home to see my girl real soon." Beep

The last message was just dead air and then a hang up.

I wonder who that was . . .

I picked up the remote control and flipped on the TV videos were on and T.I. is singing "Whatever you like" I think he is so cute and the video is so hot. As I walked to the kitchen my cell phone rings.

"Hello."

"Hey JaLisa, it's me Ramona from class."

"What's up girl you said the poetry thing starts at 9 o'clock right?"

"Yes, it does that's why . . . that's why I was calling."

"Why what's up?"

"Well I forgot to tell you that most of the people there are either gay or bi and I didn't want you to be caught off guard."

"Girl it's cool I ain't trippin . . . but can I ask you something?"

"Sure you can ask me anything."

"Ramona . . . Are you bi?"

"Yes, JaLisa I am but I'm not seeing anyone. And I'm not trying to hit on you but I thought it would be cool if we hung out."

"It's all good I'm game . . . I need to get out of this house tonight. I really don't care where we go."

"A'aight then cool so let me give you my address and we can just meet at my house and leave from here."

I wrote down the address and promised to be at her house by 8:30. I got off the phone I went to the fridge and pulled out the container of potato salad that I brought from Publix and had it with some Ritz crackers. After eating I went and turned on the shower wrapped my hair and tied it up but before I stepped in the shower I looked at my reflection in the mirror and rubbed my hand down my stomach sometimes the thought that I would never be able to conceive again frightens me. As I step into the shower my mind wanders back to Ramona's lips as I allow the water to beat on my back. I shaved my legs until they felt numb then I shaved my p---- I made sure I got it real close I could hear the phone ringing and instead of jumping out I let the machine pick it up.

~ RICHARD ~

The tour with Terrible T. has been going as scheduled. It's real cool being his opening act. We have been in a different city seems like every night for over a month. It's been about that long since I last seen JaLisa as well. I left a message on her machine this morning I'll be going back home to Miami in a few weeks and I need to sit her down and talk to her about Monica and the baby. She is about six months pregnant and I have to tell JaLisa before she has the baby. I know she might leave me after hearing that shit but I know she's gonna find out eventually.

I've seen Monica once since she told me she was pregnant and her stomach was starting to swell. Her breast looked like two balloons and she was glowing her face was so bright like it was meant for her to be carrying this baby. I thought she was going to be crying and upset and going through all those emotions you hear about when women are pregnant but she was real cool. I was able to meet her family and they really did seem happy to see me. She had already told them about my situation with JaLisa. When I got to Atlanta I only had two days so it went by real fast. I stayed in the Hilton and pretty much laid low the entire time she picked me up from the airport and drove me straight to the hotel so that we could talk. When we got up to my room she sat down on the bed and told me to come over to her she grabbed my hand and held it to her stomach it felt like the baby was doing flips so I got down on both knees and I put my head to her stomach and I talked to my baby for the first time.

~ JaLisa ~

Richard flew in last night and I picked him up from Miami
International Airport. Before we went to the house he wanted to
ride down to the beach so I told him that he should drive and we
switched seats.

I looked at Richard and said, "Babe is everything ok with you?"

"What you mean JaLisa, I just got back. I miss you, I miss the beach
and I have a lot on my mind. Let's just go walk and talk and get some fresh
air. I really miss this shit."

I didn't say anything I just gave him a half smile and put my hand on
his lap. I can feel the impression through his jeans and he has on boxers.

"Um" is all I can express at the moment. I don't know what he wants
to talk about but from his tone it sounds serious.

Instead of heading to South Beach we head a ways north near where
one of my favorite hotels the Dezerland Resort is although they have
changed the name it will always be the Dezerland Resort to me.

He parked the car on the side of the hotel and we walked through the
lobby. Richard saw a stack of clean towels at the back door by the pool exit
and he grabbed a couple of them.

As we walked out the back door he took my hand in his without even
looking at me. I just follow his lead. There was a cool breeze and you
could feel the seasons changing in the air. It's mid October and the nights
are amazing. As we headed through the trail to the beach you could hear
the waves rushing up on the seaside.

Richard says, "I bet the water is cold, feel how cool it is out here
tonight."

I helped him lay the towels down and sat down as close to him as I could. For a while we just sat there in silence then he said, "The moon is very bright tonight." He looked over his right shoulder and it's as if someone was shining a light on us.

It wasn't even a full moon but it was very bright. I pointed out the North star along with the big and little dippers. We spotted a couple walking along the water and they stopped to play in the water's edge.

Richard said "I want to see how it feels." So he took off his socks and shoes, rolled up his pants legs and put his feet in.

He called up to me "it feels great it's about 80°" He came back to me with a huge smile on his face. When he sat down I laid my head across his lap and I could feel him through his pants. I took a deep breath and loosened his pants, pulled his p---- through his boxers and gave him head as he looked out onto the ocean.

He said "Damn bay your mouth feels so good."

I asked him while he was still in my mouth "You like that?"

"What? Hell yeah!" I could taste his precum.

As I sucked on him I loosened my pants and he stuck his fingers between my legs. I wasn't wet yet and he knew it. He lifted me off of him and got on his belly then took my pants off and put my p---- in his mouth. I kept looking down the beach to make sure the lovebirds weren't headed our way. Before long I was cumming. I told him to come and sit back down and I got on top of him.

"Oh my god! Damn Richard you feel so good."

"Oh shit, you are so wet . . . this is some good ass shit. JaLisa you are the best. This is exactly what I need right now."

"Richard you are a freak, Oh . . . I don't believe we are on the beach having sex. You are a straight up freak."

"Yeah . . . I'm your freak. God damn, this p---- is tight. Oh shit! Right there!"

"I'm cumming Richard, please cum with me."

He did and we held each other for a moment. Then I hopped off of him and put my clothes back on. Just as we got dressed there were some people walking out to the beach but when they saw us they turned in the other direction.

We sat for a minute just taking in our surroundings and I asked him was he hungry. We agreed to go eat at this wing spot in town that is close by the house.

The drive was quick Richard knows all of the short cuts through town. He gets a kick out of avoiding the traffic lights.

He said "I feel so much better now I was so tense after getting off that plane."

We pulled into the Wing's spot and waited to be seated. I'm sure we could have found our own seat but we waited. Before we sat down I found the bathroom to try to freshen up a bit. I had sand coming out of my stretch jeans and the craziest look on my face. I was able to rinse off and gain my composure.

They were having Reggae night here which was surprising because this is the Wing spot. Nevertheless there was a live Reggae band and Richard and I looked at each other and just laughed.

I could feel my phone vibrating in my purse. I pulled it out and it was my friend Ramona. As I answered I looked across the table into Richards eyes.

"What's up girl?" I asked Ramona.

"Not too much, where you at?"

"I picked Richard up from the airport and we are at this Wing spot getting something to eat."

"Oh . . . I just hadn't heard from you and I wanted to you to go out with me tonight."

"Not tonight girl . . . now I'm all booed up. I'll call you tomorrow."

"Awight." She said then hung up.

Richard gave me a puzzled look. He asked "Who's that Jasmine?"

"No . . . this girl from my class Ramona, she wanted me to hang with her tonight. We've been going to this lounge down South Beach and she is hooked."

"Oh that sounds cool . . . what type of music they play?"

"Everything it's a mixture . . . they have poetry readings and its real laid back in there."

"Cool . . ."

The waitress came and took our order as we sat and listened to the band play. I occasionally listen to Reggea but Ramona is big on it.

Richard seemed real relaxed as he looked around and laughed at the band a few times. He was real amused by the live band at the wing spot.

He said, "A lot has changed since I've been away on tour with Terrible T.

"How long are you in town for Richard?"

"I'm actually here for two weeks, then I have to fly back to New York to start recording again but I'm thinking bout talking to Terrible T to see if I can do some recording here in Miami. That way I can stay here longer and just go back up as he needs me. The tour is over but there are some promotional events that I know he wants me to attend coming up soon."

"I am so happy you are here Richard. I really needed to see you, with you being away so long you felt so distant."

The food came and it was so good just as I had remembered. I don't come here without Richard because he likes this spot so I just usually put something together at home or grab something to eat from school or Publix.

~ RICHARD ~

I'm back home in Miami with my shawty. After she picked me up from the airport we headed over to North Beach and got busy. She had that thang tight and wet just like I like it. We were supposed to go there to walk and talk so I can tell her about Monica and the baby but after seeing her I just couldn't bear to hurt her like that. I love the shit out that damn girl but I am not telling her about that right now.

I got Terrible T on the phone as soon as we got to the crib and let him know I won't be back in two weeks this is going to take more time than that. He assured me that his assistant would call me with the name of the studio and who I needed to talk to when I get there. After talking to him all I could do was take a shower and crash JaLisa sucked the life out of me, had a nigga toes curling in the sand and shit.

She's up pacing the floor walking back and forth. I heard her on the phone a couple of times but I was too exhausted to get up and see what' she was talking about.

That life in New York is so fast paced and here it's much more laid back. It's just chill I'm so glad to be home. Tomorrow I'm gonna go see a few folks and make some connections while I'm here in town. With the tour and all I've become so disconnected with all that's happening here in town.

~ JaLisa ~

Richard passed out, I know he's tired from the flight and all but he is knocked out. I really missed him and I'm glad he's back. My house just feels empty without him here. Even though I've been hanging out and all it's nothing like coming home to an empty house when you are use to being home with someone.

My phone rings and interrupts my thoughts it's Mama . . .

"What's up Ma?"

"Did you pick Richard up? How was his flight?"

"Yes Ma, he's asleep, he said he was exhausted from all the running."

"Yeah, I bet he is . . . I want you to tell him I'm making dinner for him over here tomorrow and I want ya'll to come over."

"Okay Ma I'll let him know. What do you want me to bring?"

"Just your selves and an appetite."

"Okay Ma, love you see you tomorrow."

"Good night baby."

I sat looking at the phone after she hung up. She still calls me baby that's funny. I love my Mama so much but she is something else. She just wants to get Richard over there to ask him 101 questions.

When I hung up with Mama I called Jasmine to let her know to come over to Mama's house tomorrow because we are having a dinner for Richard. She said she would meet us over there and she's bringing some drinks. She know that my Mama love to drink Verde and they always have it on sale and Publix.

I called Ramona and she sounded distracted. It took her a couple of rings before she picked up.

"Hello . . ." she said.

"What's up girl. I just got off the phone with my Mama and she is doing a dinner for Richard tomorrow. I thought this would be a perfect time for you to meet him. Do you want me to pick you up at about 5 o'clock"

"Nah I'm good . . . If it's okay I'm going to have my friend Mark bring me. He'll get a big kick out of meeting Richard."

"Mark, who's that, I've never heard you mention him before?"

"He's cool we've been friends for a couple of years I ran into him when I was at the mall the other day and we've been talking since."

"Oh . . . what does he do?"

"He plays basketball overseas and he's here because they are on break. Girl he's talking about taking me overseas with him."

"What? Are you serious? What do you mean, you're in school?

"JaLisa relax I'm not talking about moving, just visiting."

"Oh . . . okay well I guess, so call me tomorrow. You remember how to get to my Mama's house right?"

"Yeah I remember that good food she cooks. I will never forget how to get over there."

When I hung up with Ramona I had to check myself. I don't know why the hell I was so annoyed about this Mark guy. She needs a boyfriend because we have been spending a lot of time together and with Richard back and all it may be for the best.

~ RICHARD ~

When I finally woke up the clock read 12:15pm it's afternoon man. I ain't slept like that in years. I called out to JaLisa but she didn't answer. There's a note by the clock.

Richard,

I didn't want to wake you. You looked so peaceful. I made some breakfast and put it in the microwave for you. Mama is doing a dinner at 5pm so whatever you have to do please have it done by then. I totally forgot that I have a meeting with the Senior Editor at the local paper 'The Sun' I will explain everything later. Keys to everything are on the dining room table.

Love,

J

I held the letter to my chest and shook my head. Damn I love this girl. Pancakes and eggs is what she had for me to eat, she knows I don't eat any red meat or pork.

I found my cell phone in the pocket of the jeans I had on last night. There were 10 missed calls and 7 messages. I don't believe I slept that long. The first two were Terrible T's assistant Trish, she left the info for the studio then she got cut off so she called back to finish the message. I have two days to get over there and start laying tracks. Everything I need will be provided by the manager when I get there. The next message was Monica she called three times said she just wanted to hear my voice and she didn't understand why I haven't called her back yet.

I just scratched my head and took a deep breath.

The rest of the calls were from friends that knew I made it back home. I'll call them sometime tomorrow.

I dialed Monica, she answers and says, "Hi, I miss you, the baby misses his daddy and I need to see you."

"Monica, I'm in Miami. I thought we were gonna be cool about this."

"Yeah I thought so too until he came and I feel like I'm going this all alone."

"Monica, you said . . ."

"Richard I don't care what I said he's here now and I'm telling you what I feel and you talking about some shit I said when I was pregnant and hormonal.'

"I'm sorry Monica, I'm so sorry what do you want me to do?"

"I want you to come spend time with your son."

"Okay Monica just give me a few days, I have a studio session set up in a couple of days and I will let you know after that. Until then I'm going to transfer some money into that account that I set up for ya'll. Take some of it and do something nice for yourself. It sounds like you are going through that post partum depression you were telling me about."

"You might be right Richard, they said the baby is colicky and he just keeps crying. I don't' know how much more I can take."

"See if your mother or sister can take the baby for a while to give you a break and I promise as soon as I can get there I will. Kiss my little man for me and tell him his daddy is on the grind for him."

For a minute I just sit here, I don't know how long I can keep this up. Somebody's gonna get hurt and I'm too deep in this thing with JaLisa to lose her now. I love my little man but I'm not in love with Monica. She is expecting more from me than I can give. I'm just gonna have to tell her the truth before she finds out on her own and then really go off on my ass.

I'm gonna have to get Monica's ass a baby sitter cause she needs to get out of that damn house. She about to blow up my spot because she so damn unhappy right now. She wound up having the baby earlier than expected and he was even premature. He only weighted 4 pounds at birth and could fit in one of my hands.

~ JALISA ~

My meeting with 'The Sun' went great I am so excited for the opportunity. I was supposed to get and internship but they offered me a Junior freelance position not only for the newspaper itself but also for their online publication. This is a great start for me to get my foot in the door. I always wanted to travel around the world writing and doing research.

Mama called me twice while I was in my meeting first she wanted to know what time I was coming then she called to find out if I could pick up the drinks. I also got a call from Terrible T his call came at the end of the meeting so I politely excused myself and took the call.

"What's up girl? I haven't heard from you since ol boy been back in town."

"I know T it's been real crazy with Mama planning this party tonight and I had a meeting with this local news paper they decided to give me a freelance position instead of an internship. I'm just leaving the meeting now you're the first to know."

"Damn Boo that's great I am so proud of you. So who are you gonna write your first article on?"

"I don't know T, I haven't even thought that far out yet."

"Well how about me? That will give me an excuse to come down and see you."

"T what do you want me to say? You know I want to see you but Richard is here, how are you going to pull that off? I really do miss you and would love to spend some time with you."

"Well I'm glad to hear you say that because I'm gonna have Richard tied up in the studio in a few days so make the most with your time with him now then he's gonna be doing a bit of traveling."

"T are you serious? He just got here!"

"Yup he's in high demand and he makin that paper."

"I know T but damn he just got here . . ."

"You'll have plenty of time to spend with him when he comes back from tour in Europe. He and my girl are going to be over there as well she's shooting a movie so I'll have you all to myself."

"Wow T all I can say is wow . . . so I'll wait for your call when you come to town. I already know you'll have everything planned out."

All I can do is shake my head Terrible T is a mess I know he's coming down and he always come correct. I don't have to do any planning all I have to do is be ready when he says the time.

I showed up to Mama's house at about 4pm to make sure I had time to help her set up. My phone went off again and Terrible T texted me a smiley face I caught a chill through my entire body. I had to close my eyes for a minute jut to gather my thoughts.

JaLisa and Chanel showed up just before 5 with more liquor and drinks then we would ever be able to consume in one night. She brought three bottles of Verde' for Mama different flavors and told her to put two up for herself when she's home alone. Chanel was friendlier I guess because she knew the party was for Richard and she could stop worrying about anything she thought Jasmine and I had.

Ramona and Mark came in a little after 5 and she is wearing my favorite lip gloss again. She had a huge smile on her face. I swear Mark must have tapped that because since we met I've never seen that look in her eyes. Mark is about 6'4 and very fair skin he has curly black hair and is so handsome. He was very respectful and kept saying yes Ma'am to Mama and she just ate that up.

Richard came at about 5:30 and Mama gave him the biggest hug, I saw his eyes water as he laid his head on her shoulder. When Mama finally let go I grabbed him by the elbow and introduced him first to Chanel which was looking a bit relieved to see that he had finally arrived. Ramona and Mark were next, Mark gave Richard a hood hand shake and they hit it off well.

They talked about Mark being overseas and playing basketball and the tour that Richard was on. They also discussed how Richard was going to be in the studio this week and even exchanged numbers because Mark would like to come to the studio to watch Richard lay down some tracks. This is off season for Mark and he will resume with practice in a couple of months.

The party was a success and Mama was real happy and a bit tipsy before we left. Richard promised her that he would be back to see her after he spent a few days in the studio and all I could think about was Terrible T and what on earth he could have planned for us here in Miami while Richard is here.

~ RICHARD ~

I really enjoyed myself at JaLisa's mom's house. The hug she gave me reminded me of the one she gave me at the hospital when JaLisa lost the baby. I had to get myself together because all I could think about was how she is going to react when JaLisa finds out about my little man in Atlanta.

Jasmine's got a girlfriend and I didn't even know she went that way. I guess that explains why she used to give me them dirty looks over JaLisa or maybe I'm just trippin. That nigga Mark said he got game I may have to catch one of his games while I'm touring overseas. He and his chick Ramona said they gonna roll through the studio and that's cool as long as they don't be in there star struck. I'm sure I'm not gonna be the only one in there laying tracks if I know Terrible T. He does everything big, I know "T" been in the game longer than I have but some shit he be over the top with I'm more of a basic dude more low profile not to flashy at all.

*   *   *

Studio time came quicker than I thought. The assistant hooked me up with the Miami Beach Recording Studio on Lincoln Road near South Beach.

The studio has a live room for vocals, voice-overs and bands along with high end recording gear to get the best in analog warmth and digital recording.

I'm hype Trish T's assistant sent over original beats and I could hear the lyrics and melodies in my head. The studio offered to prepare chord and music arrangement but I already have everything I need I just have to spit the vocals. Since I've been working with Terrible T I have not written anything on paper, he taught me to keep it all in my head. He says you get a better flow and nobody can steal your shit that way.

I came up with this one track about my girl JaLisa and how I was going to tell her about Monica and the baby. I keep going over it again and again in my head the hook is tight but I know she is not going to like it at all.

~ JALISA ~

When I woke up, Richard had already left out for his studio session. He told last night that I may not see him for a couple of days because he had a lot of work to do and needed to focus. So when my phone rang I thought it was him but remembered that he said he would be grinding out.

"Hello"

"What's up girl, I'm here I spoke with Richard and he's in the studio right now. I'm picking you up from your crib in 30 minutes. Pack light cause we gon be gone for a couple of days. I've got you all to myself and that n---- ain't even gonna have time to miss yo ass."

"What? T it's 10 in the morning . . . What do you mean a couple of days? How am I gonna explain that?

"Look I told you I was gonna be here, I'm here and you going with me. I'm picking you up myself and now you got 29 minutes you're wasting precious time."

Terrible T hung up the phone.

I don't believe this shit but I know he's on his way if he said he was in town. I jumped out the bed and ran to the bathroom brushed my teeth and turned the shower on. What does he mean pack light? I have so my thoughts going through my head. I took a quick shower and was so glad that I had shaved the day before that would take too much time. When I got out the shower I wrapped myself in a towel and headed to my closet. On one of my trips to New York I brought this red over night duffel bag that I saw in the window of this little black owned store. I look crazy scrambling and throwing clothes in this bag. I have no idea where we are going so I just put a hand full of underwear, two nigh ties, two of my favorite Victoria Secret bras, two bathing suits, two dresses, a pair of jeans and two tank tops. I have a travel kit with my deodorant and all that stuff in it. This shit is crazy . . .

When I finished all that I quickly got dressed and put on a tank dress and some sandals. I also threw a couple pair of sandals and slid some shoes in my bag. When my door bell rang I nearly jumped out of my damn skin. It was T, as I jumped in his arms I looked past him and he's pushing a black and gray brand new Bentley.

"Hello beautiful." He said.

"T where the hell are we going? Damn I missed you. I can't believe you are actually here. Come in I'm almost ready."

He stepped in but I knew we wasn't comfortable. Richard's T-shirt and shoes were in the living room and he just put his head down.

I grabbed my bag and he took it off my shoulder. I made sure everything was turned off and went back into the bathroom to get my flat iron I can't be no where looking set up. T would not tell me where we were going. He took the bag and put it in the trunk of the car and opened the passenger door. I slid in and the seats felt amazing against my thighs and ass. There is state of the art everything inside and outside of this machine. I smiled because when the car started Trey Songz was playing "Can't be friends." He is too much, we drove through the city and he didn't have a lot to say but when we pulled into the Opa Locka Airport I was like what the hell. T where the hell are we going? All he said was "I got you baby."

"I've never been on a private plane before."

"Nah boo this ain't nothing fancy this flight is only about 45 minutes to an hour where we are going."

I was so nervous, I've only been on commercial flights. We didn't even park the car we drove right up to the propeller plane and the pilot helped us in. It was just me, T and the pilot and I'm not gonna lie I was scared as shit, my mamma would kill me if she knew any of this. The pilot headed south and T put his hand on my shoulder and told me to calm down. In no time we were landing at a small airport in Key West. I have not been to the Keys since I was a little girl. My daddy drove mamma and I on the 7 mile bridge and it damn sure didn't take us no 45 minutes.

~ RICHARD ~

I got a text from JaLisa hours ago saying she was going to be away on a writing assignment for a few days and if I needed her that I should give her a call. Honestly I didn't even know my phone went off I've been so caught up in this studio. I've been going at it for hours and taking breaks only to drink water and use the bathroom. The tracks that T's assistant sent over are on fire.

I was able to finish spitting the verses for the cut about JaLisa and Monica and I know that n----- are going to be able to relate to that shit no doubt. I haven't spoken to Monica in a couple of days but I let her know I was going to be out of touch for a few days because of this studio time. The track that I spit of her and JaLisa it's deep you can hear a bit of the piano playing in the back ground and I have this feeling it's going to be epic.

I'm feeling wired right now like I can go on for days. When I walked back into the booth after taking a brief break I stepped up to the mic no paper or notes in hand just feeling like I've come in off a meditation. I put the headphones on and my head begins to rock to the instrumentals. I feel the beats running through my veins like a heroin addict. I'm higher than life as I point to the sound gut to turn the music up. Again I'm spitting as if my life depended on it. This time I'm talking about my time on tour with Terrible T, how I started off with the four other artist in New York and after doing that little premiere my world just changed in a blink of an eye. The stacks of cash, radio interviews, press releases, videos this ain't about bragging but my audience has to know this has been the most amazing year of my life. Ain't none of this shit made up this is my life and

I'm spitting the real shit of how I'm living it. By the time the track ended I was still flowing.

Thinking back on us being in New York to overseas back to New York, around the country now in my hometown of Miami where it all started and to do it all over again. Funny how life has a way of putting you back where you started. This time seeing my town with a new fresh set of eyes, with the money and connections that I have now. It's not too many places in the city where I can't go or have access too.

~ JaLisa ~

We landed at a small airport in Key West the southern most point of Florida and when we got off the plane I swear the same car that we drove to the airport in Opa Locka was sitting outside the plane but T told me they were rented and identical.

He said that he didn't put those types of miles on his personal cars so he rents when he is away from home. This time when he turned on the music Omarion's song "O" was playing "girl I'm gonna take you some place you've never been, show you some things you can tell your friends." I feel weak I don't know if it's from the plane ride or this intoxicated feeling that I have right now.

I asked "T, how did you plan all this?"

He laughed "You know I got money and people. That's all I need to say. Just sit back and relax while I take us to our destination."

I just shook my head. I didn't say another word as we drove away from the airport and down a back street. About ten minutes later we were pulling into this private two story beach house. We parked and walked up to the front door but before we walked in there was this over sized tropical potted plant by the front door with a stone laid on the dirt and T reached in grabbed the stone or so what I thought was a stone. He opened it and a set of keys were waiting there for us. He smiled and still I don't believe any of this. He effortlessly open the door with the key and led me inside the house. From the front door you could see clear through the house no neighbors and miles of ocean as far as you can imagine.

I was drawn to the over sized balcony windows I could see the water it's an aqua blue not like Miami more pure with whiter sand. There is not a cloud in the sky. When I came back to my senses I turned to T and asked, "How, I mean really."

Everything in the house is modern and appeared to be right off a showroom floor. Just looking around I thought the furniture alone throughout the house is worth a million dollars. As we walked through the place my eyes teared up because I saw several bouquets of long stemmed calla lilies. He remembered that is my favorite flower.

I turned to him and fell into his arms. He kissed me on my forehead and said "J, you mean the world to me. I want to change my life for you. I have so much love for you and I know that I can make you the happiest woman in the world."

He grabbed my hand and laid it on his chest where his heart beats and said, "I want you to wake up next to this heartbeat as often as possible."

I'm melting he took my hand again and led me outside the glass door to the deck. There we sat in the oversized wicker chairs with off white plush cushions. T pulled his chair in front of mine and looked me directly in the eyes and said, "This is only the beginning of the next chapter in our lives. There is nothing at this point that I wouldn't do for you. I know this shit is complicated right now but it won't always be like this. I came all this way to look into your eye, hold you in my arms and allow you to see that there is a world just waiting to be seen by you."

I leaned over and kissed him so passionately. The weather here is so mystical the temperature is only about 80⊠ here today but there is a light wind coming off the ocean and I can feel the moisture in the air. When I pulled my lips away from his he stood up and scooped me out the chair and laid me on this outside wicker bed. The cushions are as plush and soft as the chair I was just on. Oh my . . . he's pulling my panties off but leaving on my tank dress his hands are so warm feels like he has on heated gloves.

T starts to taste me as my body cums over and over for him. I said to him, "T this is some freaky shit," as I smiled. He looked up at me and found my spot again, "Oh T" he then got up and took off his shirt leaving on his wife beater. He unbuttoned his pants took them off with his boxers and got on top of me lifting my ass up and entering in me so deeply. I am soaking wet and cumming already. He sucked on my neck and then my nipples, again on my neck. T was grinding on me and although he felt like he was going to break something the pain felt so good. "Oh T," I said. It wasn't long before we were both cumming.

Once he came he pulled out and laid on my chest. For a moment all you could hear were the crashing of the waves. I tapped him on the back and said, "baby I have to wipe off." He lifted himself off me and gently kissed my lips. We picked clothes off the floor and stepped back into the house. I followed T upstairs and he took our bags with us. It was funny looking at his tight butt and masculine legs walking up the steps. There were five bedrooms upstairs each with its own bathroom and we shared the master suite. T dropped my bags at the foot of the king sized canopy bed and I followed him into the bathroom. It was the size of my living room with his and her sinks on opposite sides of the bathroom. There is a Jacuzzi bathtub and the shower has two huge shower heads. Instead of taking a shower T walked over to the Jacuzzi and filled it with hot water and lavender scented bath soap that was on the edge of the tub.

A flash of Richard came to mind and I remembered him giving me a bath over a year ago. I closed my eyes and shook the thoughts out of my head. For a moment I felt like the worst girlfriend in the world. T helped me into the tub. He sat in the back and sat me in the front of him between his legs. He sucked on the back of my neck and I felt wet even though I was in the water. He whispered in my ear, "Why don't you ever call me by my name, sometimes I would like for you to just say it?"

I responded by turning to face him and straddling him. I slide him inside of me and said, "Oh Terrance this is your p---- even if it is just for a couple of days. Baby it's all yours and I'm gon make sure you don't forget it." There was enough room in this tub for two more people but we were all over it. He lifted me off him before he came and leaned me over the tub lifting my ass out of the water and pounding me from the back. "Oh shit Terrance, I'm coming . . . Oh shit . . . I love you!" We both came and went back to our original position with my back towards him. I could feel the soap stinging my insides but in no way did I want to leave his arms.

The steam from the Jacuzzi knocked us both out. We didn't even get dressed after we dried off there were Terri cloth white bathrobes hanging up in the walk in closet. We put them on and closed the blinds in the room and got in the bed. It's just after 2pm and we're laying down for a nap.

*　　*　　*

A little after 6pm I woke up in T's arms and his body was generating so much heat. I turned around to face him and said, "Hey babe we've got to get something to eat."

He looked up and smiled and said, "I got you but we need to get up and get dressed." By the time we headed out the door it was 7 o'clock and the ocean turned from blue to black. It's so dark already and we missed the sunset, I'm hoping we can catch the sunrise. We got into the car and T drove us in town I don't know if he's been here before but he sure seemed real familiar.

We pulled up into this Bistro and you could smell the food coming out the door or I was just hungry as hell. I tried to get out the car and T put his hand out across my chest and asked me to wait for him so I did. He opened my door and waited for me to get out. My heart melted, I love this type of shit from him but this was only the beginning. When we walked to the door of the restaurant I noticed it was only lit by candles with just one person there to open the door and the cook.

"Terrance, did you plan this? Oh my God, are you serious?"

There was one table in the center of the restaurant with a white linen table cloth and two white candles. Our food was already prepared. We started off with salad and some of the best bread I have ever tasted. There was this oil that the chef poured into a dish with herbs mixed in it.

For my main dish I was served lobster, shrimp, scallops with noodles and a delicious cheese sauce and T had lasagna. The food smelled so good and the taste was even better. For desert we were both served strawberry cheesecake. I can admit I was so impressed. I have never experienced anything like this in my life and I want to live like this forever. I did not know he had all this planned but should I have expected anything less?

When we got back to the beach house I could barely move. We both sat in front of the TV and T turned the channels until he found us a movie. Justin Timberlake's movie was on Friends with Benefits and I looked at him and laughed and asked, "So is that what we are?"

It took him a minute before he answered but he said, "JaLisa I believe we are more than that. I want you to be my girl or shall I say my woman. At this point it's up to you. I've never felt like this for another woman before, this is really unusual for me. I can't say that I've never cheated on my girl before but I will tell you for sure that I've never fallen in love with any other woman like this. It pains me to know that you are going back home to Richard. I know he don't deserve you. He don't even know what to do with a woman like you. I look at him like a kid. You deserve a man like me, someone that really knows how to treat a woman like you."

"Terrance I love you, but I don't know what else to say."

He just shook his head and held me so close to him while we watched the rest of the movie. We actually fell asleep right there on the couch right in front of the TV.

*   *   *

Morning came quickly and I left T there on the couch sleeping. I went to the bathroom to wash my face and brush my teeth. When I walked back through the living room I left out the patio door but before I left out I grabbed my phone out of my purse. There were five missed calls and three voice messages. I walked down the back deck and went out to the ocean and stood there allowing the waves to wash over my feet until they got to my ankles.

Richard is on my mind and after talking to T last night and spending the day with him it feels like I'm outgrowing Richard. I know he's younger than I am but I have so much love for him. He asked me to marry him but we still have not come up with a date and at this point I don't even know if I'm ready for marriage, maybe in about 10 years but not now. I feel like I'm just coming into my own and I don't want to be over shadowed by his career and his successes. I honestly think I want to be single. Take some time for me to really get to know who I am. I want to start traveling the world and focus on writing. I can't see myself sitting around waiting for my man to come off tour. Before I left with T, Richard just seemed to be off. Things just felt different between us. I don't know if it's because he's been gone awhile or has he been seeing someone else. He could possibly know some shit is up with me and T. I really can't put my finger on it but it ain't right and I need to figure all this shit out when I get back.

I looked out into the ocean and I just felt a calmness come over me. I breathed in the moisture and exhaled it out. T missed the sunrise this morning and it was amazing.

When I gathered my thoughts I went back into the house and T was still asleep on the couch. I found some breakfast food in the kitchen so I made us some waffles out of pancake mix, scrambled eggs and sliced some cantaloupe. I don't know who stocked the fridge but it's here so I assume it's for us to eat. As I began to set the table T walked up behind me and he had already gotten up to brush his teeth. He startled me by kissing me on the back of my neck. My entire body shook inside. He lifted me off the floor by my waist and sat me on the counter.

"Terrance I made breakfast for you."

He said "But what if I want you for breakfast?"

"Baby I'm still sore from yesterday."

He began to suck on my neck and moved down my breast. My breathing got so heavy and I didn't stop him nor did I want to. T cleared off the counter and slid off my panties. I'm at a loss for words. We were in action right there on the counter and he said, "We can heat the breakfast up in the microwave."

I didn't say another word about the food. At this point I'm soaking wet and my ass is being lifted off the counter. "Oh Richard" almost came out of my mouth between moans but I caught myself and "Oh Terrance," came out. We are knocking shit on the floor and everything. We both came and I couldn't move so I just lay back on the counter and closed my eyes. T went to the bathroom brought me back a warm rag then he said, "Now we can eat."

We decided to go eat out on the back deck so that we could see the ocean. It is absolutely breath taking and this never gets old to me. I could spend my days and nights looking out onto the ocean.

T said, "As much as I'm enjoying you I have to get back to New York she sent me a message that we needed to sit down and talk. She said it's a sit down face to face conversation that she doesn't want to have over the phone."

I can't even imagine what she wants to discuss. It could be about the business or the tours, anything. My expression changed because even thought I know that we would have to leave eventually and I would have to go home and face Richard I feel like I need more time.

We ate, cleaned up our mess and got dressed. T drove us back to the airport that we flew in at and the pilot took us back to Opa Locka. T drove back to my house and for some reason my eyes welled up I am feeling so many emotions. He made a few calls and made sure that Richard was back at the studio. T didn't want to run into him while he was taking me home. When we pulled up in front of my house a few tears rolled down my cheek and this was only the beginning to my heart break. We hugged, kissed and said our goodbyes. We both promised to see each other soon.

When I walked in I dropped my bags at the door and sat on one of the bar stools in front of my kitchen. I took my phone out of my purse and began to check the missed calls surprisingly none of them were from Mama. All of the missed calls were from a 404 Atlanta area code but I don't recognize the phone number. The first message was a young lady by the name of Michelle she said, "Hi, um JaLisa I know you don't know me but I'm Monica's sister and I need to speak with my as soon as you get this message."

I don't know anyone in Atlanta with either one of those names but it seems they know me.

The second message was Michelle calling back, "Listen JaLisa I'm sorry to bother you but please call me back I have something very important that I think you should know about Monica and Richard."

I took the phone away from my ear before I could listen to the last message so that I could dial the number back. Michelle answered on the first ring and before I could say a word she said, "JaLisa I need you to hang up I'm going to send you something then I will call you right back. She then hung up and a few seconds later I received a picture of a beautiful baby boy and damn if he don't look just like Richard's baby pictures.

My phone rang and it was Michelle she said, "Listen I hate to be the one to tell you this but Richard and my sister Monica had this baby and she's told me about you and him. I think that you should know that he has been seeing her and sending them money. My problem is not him doing for them but that my sister has been sitting here crying for days over this man that is sleeping with her unprotected. Then going back to Miami and I'm sure he is not protecting himself with you."

All I could say to Michelle was thank you. My head is pounding and I can't take any more of this conversation. I politely told her that I had to go and that I would call her back as soon as I got a chance. I forwarded the picture to my email then to Richard's phone. I took my phone and smashed it against the wall pieces went flying all over the living room floor. I locked myself in my room and cried as if someone had died. I didn't even cry like this at my father's funeral. All I could think about is that I will never be able to conceive and how this must be payback for me being with T. I walked over to his dresser where his cologne, pictures and watches are and in one swoop knocked everything on the floor. I pulled all of his clothes out of the closet and drawers not even taking them off the hangers and threw them on the floor.

I opened the bedroom door and took his stuff and put it in the second bedroom. I can't stop crying I went back in the room and locked the door and the house phone began to ring. I pulled myself together and answered the phone by my bed.

"Hello," I answered.

"JaLisa, baby where did you get this picture?"

"Does it matter?"

"Why you not answering your cell?"

"Cause I broke it!"

"JaLisa, listen baby please, I'm sorry . . ."

"Your right!" was my response and I yanked the cord out the wall and smashed that phone against the wall as well. I laid down on the bed and cried until my stomach hurt. When he came home I was still locked in the room.

Richard is banging on the door.

"JaLisa please let me in."

"Go f--- yourself Richard or better yet go f--- Monica!"

"Baby I want to explain please we are better than this . . . I knew after all you went through with losing our baby I had to find the right time to tell you this."

I could hear him trying to break in the door.

I walked over to door and put my back against it and began to cry uncontrollably. I slid down to the floor with my back still against the door. I was thinking to myself that maybe this is my way out. I don't know but I never wanted things to end this way. Even though we both cheated I still do love him.

He's begging at the door now.

"Baby please . . . I need to see you. I need to hold you. I swear I never meant to hurt you or have you find out like this. Baby you are my best friend and soon to be my wife. Please JaLisa I need to see your face."

In my moment of weakness I opened the door but I was still sitting on the floor. I can't stop crying, my insides are aching and my head is pounding. Richard lifted me off the floor and held me in his arms.

He said, "Baby you are my life, I love you with all my heart and I need you. I can't lose you over this. I don't even love her. It meant nothing to me but that is my son. I know you don't deserve this, here you are holding it down for me and making sure I have a home to come to after touring.

JaLisa I need you. Baby I can't do this nor do I want to do any of this without you."

I can hardly talk I'm so hoarse.

"How? Why? When? Richard when did you and her? Wait, no I don't want to know the details. I don't believe I trusted you."

As the words come out of my mouth I want to tell him I've been f---ing his boss but he does not need to know that.

I asked him, "How am I supposed to deal with this?"

"Baby we can get through this I won't see her any more only to deal with my son. Anything you want. Whatever you need from me I'll do it just to keep from losing you."

I can't breathe. I need some time to digest this all. I asked him to let me go and I walked into the bathroom then locked the door behind me. I turned the shower on took my clothes off and stepped inside. I allow the water to wash over my body and even my hair. I'm not crying anymore and I have to pull myself together before I leave out of this bathroom. I can't allow him to see me like this. He does not get the gratification of seeing me like this.

When I came out of the bathroom he was sitting on the edge of the bed. He had tears running down his face and he looked so damn pitiful. I'm wrapped still in my towel soaking wet and he hugged me.

He said, "I'm going to go get you another phone."

He picked up the pieces of my cell from the living room and took it with him. I didn't even dress I just got in the bed after taking two Xanax that I had from when I went back to the doctors from losing the baby. I slept for hours when I finally woke up twelve hours had passed by and my headache was gone.

~ RICHARD ~

aLisa found out about Monica and the baby and she lost it. I called Monica when I left out to get JaLisa a new phone and she said that her sister got the number the last time I came up there and was just waiting to call. Although I'm glad it's finally out I damn sure didn't want my girl to find out like this.

When I came back to the house with her new phone she was asleep and has been for a very long time. I had to keep checking on her just to make sure she was still breathing . . . I saw a bottle of Xanax on the dresser and still don't know how many she actually took. I am so worried about her I hate seeing her like this.

I feel like shit for doing this to us. I had no business being with Monica. I don't even know why I did it I have such a good woman and I know she wouldn't do no shit like this to me. As she sleeping I put all my stuff back in the drawers and hung my clothes up in the closet. Some of my pictures got messed up from the cologne but what can I say. I took the towel off her and put a night gown on her and she didn't even budge. I know I should have sat her down and had this discussion with her as soon as I got back but I could never find the right words to express myself to her. I am going to be real messed up if she leaves me or put me out. Not that I can't get my own place or anything like that but this is my woman and I don't want to lose her. I realize now that she is the best that ever happened to me.

When she woke up I was laying beside her on the bed with my arm around her waist. I pulled her close to me and the warmth from her body turned me on. Damn I love this girl. I can't believe I'm lying here crying . . . I've never cried over a woman before but I know she wants to leave me. She has had enough of my shit and this just may be the last straw.

"JaLisa please baby give me another chance."

She said, "I don't want to have this discussion, not now, not today."

"I understand can I just hold you?"

She slid out of my arms and went to the bathroom. After the toilet flushed I heard the shower come on so I got her a bra and underwear out of her top drawer and laid them on the bathroom counter for her. I also hung her robe on the back of the bathroom door so that she could feel comfortable. T's assistant called me a couple of times to find out why I wasn't at the studio but I just let it roll to the voicemail. I'm going to have to make sure my girl is okay before I leave out of here.

When she got out of the shower I had her phone on the table. I showed her that I had all of her phone numbers transferred to the new phone she was also given the same number that she had before but if she wanted to change it she could. Her mother called a few times while she was sleeping and I let her know that I just told her that she was asleep.

She didn't show to much interest in the phone even though it was an upgrade with a touch screen and all. I followed her into the kitchen and she gave me a look as if to say back the f--- up. It's just that I don't know what to do or say. I felt so helpless. I want to hold her but I see she is not in the mood.

Before I could say anything else she opened the fridge and pulled out some lunch meat and ate it right out of the container. Then she grabbed a bottle of water and drank the entire thing. She didn't have much to say to me at all and I figured that this is how it would be for a while. She walked right past me into the bedroom and got dressed in a pair of jeans and tank top.

I asked her, "Where are you going?"

She said, "I have to go over to my school and then I need to stop by the paper to go over the writing that I did while I was away."

"Do you want me to take you?"

She responded, "No I'm good, don't you have to be at the studio right now?"

"I do . . . I'm supposed to but I want to be here for you."

"Listen Richard I'm a grown woman, I'm good. I've had my good cry and I'm ready to move on."

I watched as she put her shoes on grabbed her school bag, purse and literally walked out the front door. I feel like such a bitch right now . . . like I want to chase behind her and profess my love.

~ JaLisa ~

As soon as I got in the car I pulled out my new phone and called T. The phone rang a couple of times before he answered.

He said, "Hi baby how are you?"

"I'm okay," was all I could muster up.

"I'm glad you called I needed to talk to you about why she had me come back to New York."

I said, "Okay."

He began, "I don't know how to tell you this but she found out that she is two months pregnant and she waited to tell me because she had a miscarriage a couple of years ago and she wanted to make sure before she got all excited."

I honestly don't know what he said after that because I took my new phone and tossed it out the driver side window. When I looked back in the rear view mirror a Mercedes truck on the opposite side of the street crushed it with its front right tire.

Today I begin a new chapter in my life and I AM SINGLE!!!!!

The End

ACKNOWLEDGEMENTS

To my beautiful daughters Alexia Etheridge and Diamond Fowler all that I do is for the both of you. From the time I roll out of bed until I pass out at night know that I do it all for you!

To my grandmother Shirley "Pooh Bear" Mitchell you have always been an inspiration to me and I love you for that thank you for never giving up on me. I know that you are smiling down on me from heaven and will always be with me wherever my travels take me. To my mother Deborah Lorraine Parker and my brother Patrick Lamont "Tuffy" Diggs wow it's been over ten years since the both of you have become my angels and not a million words in a million books will ever be able to begin to explain how much I miss you both. I remember you telling me that *"you are going to miss me when I'm gone"* and you spoke nothing but truth when you used to tell me that . . . To our family and many friends in the DC metropolitan area we know that you miss us and our presence but just know that we are here in Florida living the life. We've been through hurricanes, had tough times, and it was such a blessing to see how you all pulled together for us. We will never forget that and we want you to know that we love you all for your support and encouragement. On that same note please stop trying to move in!!!! I want to give special thanks Brandi Pressley and the staff at ABLE Office Services for their continuous hours of editing and advice. I would also like to give thanks to Valerie Carter and Victoria Hester for their editing as well just when I thought I was finished they both took another look and we did it over again. Again thanks because I know that you didn't have to. To Ashley Coley, Shanique Rozier and all of my family and friends I miss you more and more every single day.